Love in Time of War

"Natalie had never thought of the possibility of being bombed on the street and she put the idea out of her mind at once. She knew such fears were dangerous, even if there were a grain of truth in them. 'There is nothing to fear but fear itself,' went through her mind and she clung to it. The men on the field had a right to such fear, but even they put it aside when the chips were down.

"She stared into the crowd, seeking Johnny, and she heard the cries growing lower and the voices diffusing into talk. . . .

"A siren began to whine in the distance, and faces turned around with looks of alarm. Lee caught a glimpse of Johnny under a street light, talking to the men who held the girls, and everyone was turning in the direction of the siren's whine."

Vietnam Nurse

Della Field

AN AVON BOOK

AVON BOOKS
A division of
The Hearst Corporation
959 Eighth Avenue
New York, New York 10019

First Avon Printing, September, 1966

Cover illustration by Mort Rosenberg

Printed in the U.S.A.

CHAPTER 1

One October day the *S.S. Charity* drew into the port of Saigon, where small and large boats were clustered. The shore was green after the recent monsoons and trees shimmered in the afternoon sun. The *Charity* had been at sea for weeks, following the example of its sister ship *Hope*. It had passed through good and bad weather on the Pacific, but every day except Sunday had been spent by the ship's two hundred passengers belowboard, at work. The *S.S. Charity* was a medical ship sent over by the U.S. Naval Corps; it contained laboratories, a medical library, study rooms, and over two hundred beds. In the busy port of Saigon, it stood out—white and clean—against the muddy blue water.

Natalie Knight, an ensign in the Navy Nurse Corps, stood at the railing of the *Charity* with her navy blue cloak blown back from her white uniform, her white cap, trimmed in blue and gold, pinned to her dark brown hair. She held on tight to the railing, excited and nervous about her arrival in this strange port. All that she had learned in the past months began to fade away before the reality of this moment. Before her lay Saigon, the capital of South Vietnam, the city everyone at home was reading about in the newspapers.

Other nurses and hospital corpsmen were crowding onto the deck, with their small travelling bags in hand, eager to disembark. Most of them exclaimed about the cluttered sampans around the docks, the smell of fish in the air, the relief of seeing trees at last. But Natalie stayed by herself, as she had during the journey. Her soft brown eyes contained a deep look of determination as

5

she stepped into line and began to move away from the *Charity*. Just as she did so, four American planes roared overhead, and everyone looked up into the blue sky. Each plane left four trails of dark smoke behind it and rushed toward the horizon. It was a reminder of the war that was going on beyond the shoreline they approached, these naval officers in their blue trims. Natalie shivered and stepped off the boat.

A row of blue navy buses were waiting for them at the edge of the shore, and the medical officers passed through clusters of Vietnamese civilians and soldiers who cheered them as they passed. Some of the officers waved back as they climbed into their buses, but Natalie tried not to smile with pleasure. Her face was pale with anxiety. She sat by an open window and stared out at the *Charity*, as if it were a mirage. She had to bite her lower lip to keep from crying when the bus steamed away from the port and headed toward the city of Saigon.

A balmy wind blew on her cheeks. That was her first impression. Next she was aware of a number of army jeeps and tanks on the streets outside. And, finally, she noticed the beauty of the landscape. High white buildings were only half-hidden by the trees, and the streets were wide and bordered by exotic flowerbeds. She had never seen so many different kinds of trees at once, nor so many different kinds of architecture. One building might resemble pictures she had seen of Paris, while another resembled ones she had seen of old China. Her eyes widened in surprise. From the study she had given to the diseases and wounds of this country, she had only gotten a sense of primitive living. She had never expected Saigon to be the epitome of graceful civilization.

She saw many bicycles ridden by lovely girls in colorful tunics and pantaloons (*ao-dais*) and pedicabs that looked like rickshaws but were driven from behind by tall tricycles. She saw vendors carrying baskets of goods on the ends of bending bamboo yokes and bobbing palm-leaf and straw, cone-shaped hats. Everything was colorful and gay, except for the soldiers and armed cars in dark olive green. Natalie held her breath before the general excitement of the city. She tried to keep her feelings immune from it, but the warm wind on her cheeks kept drawing her gaze to the streets of Saigon.

On the bus with her were ensigns from the Navy Nurse Corps, girls with whom she had travelled but spoken little. She looked at them now and wished she had a friend among them, but they were chattering among themselves. They ignored her, naturally, after she had ignored them for so long. She sat alone now, paying the price for her chosen solitude, and, as they neared the naval hospital, she wrote an imaginary letter home to her family and friends describing all that she was seeing.

The hospital was a huge cement building outside the center of the city. It was functional in appearance, although the new arrivals had been told that there were a swimming pool, tennis courts, and playing fields on the grounds. Tall trees grew around the building and gave a little shade to the earth. The buses drew up at a side entrance and released the passengers slowly. They were led inside and directed to their dormitory quarters at once. Their suitcases would follow them.

The antiseptic smell in the air reminded Natalie of her reason for being there, and she left that part of the hospital uneasily. The corridors were brightly lit, and she followed a group of ensigns down to an elevator that would take her to her third-floor room. She was nervous at the thought of a roommate, someone higher in rank she had been told, who would show her the ropes and make her feel at home. She wanted to be left alone.

Again, in the elevator, she was ignored by the others who exclaimed on the beauty of Saigon and their joy in being there. She watched their faces, young and lively, and saw how much hope they all had. It made her envy them against her will. She wanted to feel all right the way she was, but it was hard when she was lonely and afraid.

The third floor was white and contained several double rooms. Natalie left the group on the elevator and looked for room number thirty-seven. She walked past six rooms, containing colorful bedclothes and bright curtains, until she reached her own. She knocked on the closed door but got no reply. With a lump in her throat, she opened the door and saw twin beds, twin desks, twin bureaus, and pretty white silk curtains. One of the beds was covered by a flimsy red spread; the other contained two piles of neatly folded sheets and blankets. A navy pennant hung over the made bed and the bureau was covered with bottles of perfume and jars of makeup. A photograph of two old people stood by the mirror, as well as a photograph of a round navy lieutenant.

Natalie closed the door behind her and set her travelling bag on her desk. She removed her cloak and cap and went to the window. She had a view of a bright green playing field and the two other sides of the hospital. She saw that the sun was setting already, growing gold in the blue sky, and before she could burst into tears, she began to make her bed.

The door burst open and she jumped.

"Hi!" said a plump girl with blond curls under her cap and bright red lipstick. "I'm Maggie Jackson."

"Natalie—Knight."

"Natalie? What's your nickname?"

"Well, Lee."

"Well, Lee, glad to have you here," Maggie said with a big smile and she went to the mirror to look at herself. "Did you have a good trip?"

"It was long, but interesting," Natalie said and continued to make her bed with quick, efficient gestures, "I guess I learned a lot."

"You going to work on the ship, or here?"

"Both, I guess . . . I'll teach there and practice here."

"They're short of teachers. That's good."

Maggie flopped down on her bed and unpinned her cap. Her hands and legs were plump and brown, her figure bulged under her uniform. She sat watching Natalie—now Lee—through bright, critical eyes.

"You'll have fun here, a knockout like you," she remarked.

"I hope so," Lee said, without meaning it.

8

"You can buy all sorts of gorgeous stuff in town, you know, for almost nothing."

Lee finished the bed and sat down to remove her shoes and examine her roommate more closely.

"I guess I'll have to get a bedspread to match yours," she said, "Maybe dark blue would be nice."

"You should be sick of dark blue by now," Maggie said.

Lee rummaged in her bag for a hairbrush and began to unpin her carefully knotted hair. It fell into long rich loops around her shoulders and face, and shadowed her pale, voluptuous features. Maggie looked at her with open envy, as she brushed her hair till it snapped with electricity.

"Saigon looks really beautiful," Lee said.

"Wait till you get a taste of the other side, Doll. You'll feel different then. I've been here for three years. It's no bowl of roses."

"Do you speak the language?"

"Not very well, but I can get along. A little French too. How about you?"

"A little of both," Lee said and managed a smile. "That really scares me."

"That, and everything else. You look like a rabbit chasing a hound."

Lee smiled at her quickly. "I guess I do. I don't know where I am yet."

"We all feel like that the first few days. Relax. It'll pass."

At that moment a bell rang and Maggie jumped up.

"Food, at last," she exclaimed. "I'm starving!"

Lee put her hair back into its knot as fast as she could, but her fingers were trembling. Meanwhile, Maggie was retouching her face and re-doing her cap, and Lee prayed that she wouldn't leave her alone. For once, she wanted a companion. She clipped on her cap as quick as she could, and it turned out she had to wait for Maggie.

"Let's go," said Maggie at last, and Lee followed her into the hall.

* * *

9

The dining hall turned out to be pleasant in appearance. It didn't have the grim look of so many dormitory or institutional dining rooms, but flowers brightened the tables and the officers in their neat suits gave the room a trim air. A few people in civilian clothes were eating there, however, as well as some non-naval men. Lee was surprised to see so many Vietnamese nurses in the room. The food, served on trays, was tasty and welcome. She and Maggie sat by a window at a table for four, but they were the only ones there.

"My boyfriend—Bennie—is down at the Mekong Delta this week," Maggie said, "They're learning how to navigate the ships on inland rivers now, and I guess it isn't so easy. The VC's sneak along in sampans and junks, but they know how to maneuver them. Not like our boys."

Lee overheard a small Vietnamese nurse say to a naval doctor at the next table: "Chao Ong Bac Sy My." She was pleased to find she knew what it meant: "Hi, American Naval Doctor." But she couldn't catch any more of their conversation, because Maggie was telling her about Bennie.

"He's no hero," she was saying, "but he's efficient, you know, and his men respect him. He doesn't lose his temper or act like a bully the way the army officers do. He's good-natured and brave, a real fighter . . . I just wish he didn't have to go away so much."

"Yes. That's too bad," said Lee.

"What's that ring you've got on your finger, by the way?" Maggie asked, pointing at the diamond on Lee's left hand.

"An engagement ring."

"They ask you girls not to marry till you've served your time," said Maggie with a frown. "Didn't you know that?"

"Yes."

"So when do you plan to get married?"

"Not until I've served my time," Lee said, looking down at her plate. Her dark eyes grew moist under her thick lashes. "I guess," she added.

"What's the story? Who is he?" Maggie asked in an

10

eager voice. Now it seemed that she was relieved to find that Lee was already tied down to somebody.

"His name is Tom Lender. I've known him for ten years."

"Oh! One of those childhood-sweetheart romances. I'm surprised he let you come over here."

Lee didn't answer, but drew in her breath to control the emotions that were rising to the surface too quickly, too easily.

"Did you have a fight, or something?" Maggie persisted, fixing her gaze on Lee's lowered, lovely face.

"No," Lee murmured, "No fight."

"You just wanted to travel?"

"Sort of."

"Well, I guess you don't want to talk about it yet," said Maggie, "But no wonder you look so lost is all I can say. If you're the faithful type, it won't be much fun here after all. Just a lot of hard work."

"That's okay," Lee said.

"Bennie will be back soon. We'll take you into town one of these nights. We can cheer you up. We like to go over to the French Quarter sometimes, or to the Caravelle Bar. That's where all the newspaper men hang out, and it's kind of fun to talk to some Americans outside the service. Or sometimes we go to the Officers' Club and laugh it up with the boys from the Special Forces. Bennie has lots of Green Berets for friends."

Lee heard only half of what Maggie was saying, although she appreciated her roommate's efforts at cheering her up. She wanted to go to her room as soon as possible, to be alone with her thoughts. She had never felt so lonely before, and she couldn't eat much in spite of her hunger.

"What do you do on the nights that Bennie's away?" she asked Maggie.

"Play bridge or go to the movies. There's a movie theatre here. They show some good ones."

"I think I'll go upstairs now—I'm tired—and my bags should be there. I'd better unpack," Lee said.

"Sure. I'll help you."

11

Lee longed to say no, go away, but she couldn't. Maggie meant well, and she appreciated the effort.

They took their trays back to the counter and left the dining room. Maggie waved to several people on the way but seemed to sense that Lee wasn't ready to be introduced. She watched Lee out of the corner of her eye, curiously. Obviously it was strange for her to see someone wearing a big engagement ring and a sad face at the same time.

On the elevator, she said to Lee: "I hope you'll tell me what's on your mind, Doll, because if we have to live together, we better share our secrets. Otherwise, it'll be hell."

Lee looked unnerved, and she twisted the ring on her finger automatically. She knew that Maggie was telling the truth. It could be very grim sharing a room with a stranger, for both of them, and she longed to have a friend now. But how could she trust anyone, under the circumstances? Maybe she would just have to take the risk. She glanced at Maggie's round, generous face and put aside her doubts.

"Okay," she said. "While I unpack, I'll talk."

Maggie squeezed her hand and they went on to room thirty-seven, where the bags were indeed waiting. Both girls removed their uniforms and changed into cool bathrobes. It was dark outside by now and the sky was full of stars.

"I have an early shift tomorrow," Maggie said, settling down on her bed. "So it's lucky I'm not playing bridge."

Lee began to take out her uniforms and civilian dresses and hang them in her closet, one by one, and they made her more homesick than ever. They reminded her of her mother and father, of her little sister, of Mr. and Mrs. Lender, of her best friend Ann. She wanted to be alone, to cry, again, but Maggie was waiting.

"So, where are you from, Lee?" she asked.

"A small town in Oregon—called Oceanview—and then I went to nursing school in Portland."

"I knew a guy from Portland," said Maggie. "Real cute."

Lee turned to look at her. "Did you know him here?"

12

"Sure thing."

"Where is he now?"

"He went home."

"Tom's from Portland too—that is, after he left Ocean-view."

"Did you follow him there?" Maggie asked.

"Yes. He was at the university, and he was a couple of years older than I. I'd known him at school before and always was crazy about him. But we didn't get together till he was in Portland. Then he enlisted and went to boot camp in Texas, where I visited him once. After that, he was at Fort Benning in Georgia, and I visited there too . . . Finally he was at the JFK Special Warfare Center. We got engaged before he came over here. That was a year and a half ago."

"He was a Green Beret?" Maggie asked, her voice full of wonder.

"Yes."

"Where is he now?"

"They don't know," Lee said, turning to look at Maggie. "But I intend to find out. He was lost on the Cambodian border—just disappeared—so I'm sure he's still alive, a prisoner of war."

Maggie looked at Lee for a long time, without speaking. Then she began to shake her head very slowly, a crease between her eyebrows. Her expression showed disapproval of Lee and all that she had said.

"Forget it, Doll. Men are disappearing all the time, but the VC's let us know who the prisoners are. They use them to make deals with the government. If he hasn't turned up on their list, he's dead. Face it."

"No!" Lee cried. "I won't forget it. Sometimes they don't tell who they have for years. I know that."

She leaned into one of her bags and removed a thick packet of letters bound in red ribbon.

"These are from him," she said. "I know he's still alive . . . Here, look at my picture of him."

She drew a photograph of a handsome dark-haired man in a green beret out of the packet of letters, and she

13

handed it to Maggie. In the picture, he was smiling proudly.

"I can see why you don't want to let that one go," Maggie remarked, "He's really something . . . but I'm sorry, Lee, I think you better give up the hunt, take off the ring, and live a little . . . Did you join the Navy just to find him?"

"Yes. When they couldn't find him, I joined. I already had my nursing degree, so it only took a year to get over here. But a year is a long time, and now that I'm here, I'm more determined than ever."

"This is one for the books all right," said Maggie. "It's crazy. He's bound to be dead, Doll. I promise. I might as well be frank. I've been around here for a long time, I should know. They don't just turn up again out of the blue. It's a dream you're carrying. You must have been really crazy about him."

"I was," said Lee. "I am."

But how could she tell Maggie how much she loved Tom, how long she had watched him at school and waited for the day that he would see her. How could Maggie know the joy she felt when he smiled at her in the hall one day, and when, at last, he came to her and kissed her right on the street in Portland. It was a dream that she was carrying still; that was true. Tom was part of her adolescence, her daydreams then, part of her growing up into womanhood, and finally part of her whole future. He had lived in her imagination for many years. In a way, his disappearance didn't matter to her because he had such a strong place in her mind. She had never looked at another man with love or desire.

"Well, Lee, you're going to think I'm awfully tough," Maggie said, "but I think you've come to Saigon for all the wrong reasons. I know I'm no genius, and I don't have a quarter of your looks, but I think I'm ahead of you in one way. I see things for what they are. The rest of us are here to fight the enemy, either on the battlefield or here in the hospital. You're here for some romantic ideas that just won't mix with the facts . . . I hope you can stand up to the shock, I really do. Tomorrow you'll start

14

working with sick and wounded people. You'll be teaching ignorant folks how to treat yaws, beri-beri, malaria. And where will your dream be then?"

"Here," said Lee, and she raised her diamond to the light, where it glittered and reflected many colors in its prisms. "Right here."

"Hmph!" Maggie snorted in disbelief, and she went to the door of the room. "I'm going down the hall to play bridge with the girls. This is all too much for me and my ordinary brain."

And with that, she shut the door firmly behind her, leaving Lee alone to put her clothes away. But Lee stood in the middle of the room, not moving. Her face showed pain, and tears came to her eyes. When she did move, it was only to put the photograph of Tom on her bureau, then take it down again, and hold it against the white silk of her dressing gown. She clasped it against her breasts while tears poured down her cheeks at last.

CHAPTER 2

Lee rarely saw Maggie for the next few days. The two girls were working in separate areas. Lee had been trained for operating room management while Maggie was head nurse in a big ward at the hospital. Lee's life was divided between work in the operating room from six to twelve each morning, and the instruction of hospital corpsmen, as well as Vietnamese students, on the ship *Charity* until five each evening. It was an exhausting but exciting schedule, and Lee grew to love the daily trip through Saigon. At night she was too tired to do anything but write letters and read books from the library.

Much to her own surprise, she got up eagerly each morning, and ate a quick breakfast by herself in the dining room. In the operating room, she worked with a Lieutenant S.G., a doctor named Joe Curtis. He had been with the navy for many years, serving on the field, on ships, and finally in the dispensaries stationed around the countryside of Vietnam. He was a bachelor in his forties and a very efficient surgeon. Besides him, there was another American nurse named Joyce and a Vietnamese girl named Khai. All three were well-trained and grateful for the added presence of Lee.

"We were really understaffed in here," Joe said to Lee one morning. "I guess that's how Khai learned to do so much so fast."

"What is most of the work you have to do?" Lee inquired.

"Removal of shrapnel and suturing wounds. Most of the severe cases go by jet to Denver, Colorado. We prepare them for the journey or else get someone back to-

16

gether again . . . You'll find it's pretty routine. The trouble comes with deep wounds. How to find the stuff, you know, and get it out without hurting any of the organs. But a lot of the time there's tissue to be sutured together way inside. That's tough."

"It doesn't sound at all routine to me," said Lee, "but very hard. You must be very skilled."

"I've been around. That's all," Joe said with a smile at her.

"Do you ever treat the prisoners?" Lee asked.

"Once in awhile. But most of the Vietnamese we get are the civilians, the poor folks hammered by accident, and we only do them when their own hospital is filled. That happens sometimes . . . As the saying goes: *Da La Vien Tro My*."

"This is American aid," Lee translated aloud with a smile. "I'm finding it hard to understand the politics here."

"I don't blame you. It takes awhile to even know there's a riddle, and then that's all you have. A riddle. Nobody seems to know the answer to it."

He looked up as Khai entered the little room where they were sitting with cups of coffee. She entered shyly, as usual, although there was a look of distant conviction behind her outward gaze—a look that Lee recognized. She was a small, slim girl, with an elfin face capped by a thick crown of black hair parted in the middle. In her white uniform, she looked like a mischievous angel, and her smile was as gentle as an angel's too.

"Hello there," she said in her difficult English.

The doctor stood up and said he had to go, but he squeezed Khai's shoulder as he passed her for the door. She smiled at Lee and sat down beside her.

"He's a wonderful man, Dr. Curtis," said Khai.

"Yes. He is. He makes me want to work very hard."

"Me too. You work on the *Charity* too?"

"Yes," said Lee.

"My sister Khoung is learning medicine there. Have you seen her?"

"Not yet. I'm taking a long time learning names. It's

17

hard enough teaching for the first time," said Lee, "I get quite nervous standing up there."

"Oh, well. It's a good thing you do. It makes sense."

"Do you come from Saigon, Khai?"

"No. From a hamlet a few miles south, toward Cochin. Not a very healthy hamlet," she laughed, "but Khoung hopes to go back there to work. She wants to help with the new dispensary there. We are full of disease at home. Not like American small towns, huh?"

"Some of our Southern towns are poor too," said Lee, remembering her time with Tom in Georgia. "You'd be surprised."

"I would, yes. We hear so many beautiful things about America. I had a friend who went there to study. He's still there."

"Maybe you'll come over some time?"

"I doubt it," said Khai. "My work is here. I have great pride in my country. I would like to show you Saigon some time, if that is all right with you."

"I'd love it! Thank you," said Lee.

"Girls don't go out alone at night, but during the day . . ."

"Well, I might be able to arrange for us to go out one night with a couple here," Lee suggested. "Then we could do it in the day too."

"*Tot Lam*," said Khai with a smile. It meant "Very nice."

A few minutes later they were called to work. They washed their hands and put on their gloves and masks before entering the operating room. Dr. Curtis entered from his private room, and Joyce wheeled in the patient through the swinging doors. The room was brightly lit and smelled of anesthesia. Joyce was a skilled anesthetist, and she had already dulled the patient's pain with morphine. The patient was a middle-aged Vietnamese woman who had two broken collar bones. Her face was cut as well. Her eyes were open and Joyce immediately applied ether while the doctor examined the woman's chest.

"What happened?" he asked Joyce from behind his mask.

"A riot outside City Hall."

"Bad?"

"Not yet."

The doctor said, "Why isn't she undressed yet?"

"No time," said Joyce.

He nodded at Khai and Lee, who immediately drew back the sheets and began to remove the woman's *ao dai*. Its pretty blue color was spattered with blood, and the girls glanced at each other over their masks. The patient was still writhing with pain, or the reaction to it, but her head began to nod drowsily against the dose of ether. Khai removed her pantaloons and stopped. She looked at Lee and then at the doctor.

"She's pregnant," she said, "Many months."

Dr. Curtis went to feel her stomach and nodded his head at Khai. It seemed that the woman was about to give birth.

"You deal with that," he said to Lee with a nod at the woman's stomach. "I'll deal with this."

They all gave out small laughs and began to apply themselves to the job of delivering a child while setting a cast for broken bones. Luckily the woman had given birth before—probably several times—and it was a very simple matter. While Khai and Lee watched the stomach contractions, Joyce and the doctor took an X-ray of the chest and discovered the bones could be set in a simple cast, without operating.

A couple of hours passed very quickly and a nurse entered to say there was a new patient from the riot, another civilian, waiting outside. No sooner had she announced this than a new baby made its appearance in the world with harsh screams and wiggles. Khai held it up—a little boy—her eyes smiling over her mask. She then put it over her arm for a nasty spank. Lee watched the baby and felt like crying with a mixture of laughter and tears. The doctor cut the cord and they all gathered around to look at the tea-colored infant.

"Okay. Take care of him, Khai," Dr. Curtis said. "Roll her away, Joyce."

And in a few minutes the operating room was ready for

another patient, this time a young boy with a fractured skull.

And this was a typical morning for Lee. If it got to be noon, and she was in the middle of an operation, her shift would enter and take her place. She always left reluctantly. She was absorbed by this work and anxious to help the wounded soldiers, sailors, and civilians who came into the operating room. It was her only contact with the war, about which she knew very little. What she had read in the papers was so ambiguous and hard to understand that she had given it up as a loss. What she had heard from Tom when he wrote from Vietnam was also unreal to her—tales of parachuting, guerrilla fighting, flying. But she began to be curious about the cause of all the suffering she saw, and she was also curious to see Saigon in detail.

One evening she came home and found Maggie all dressed up in a bright green dress, her blond hair newly set.

"Bennie is back," she said.

"That's wonderful!" said Lee. "Where will you go to celebrate?"

"To the officers' club. Lots of men are in this time." She fluffed and teased her hair in front of the mirror and spoke to her reflection, "We're going out for dinner first."

"That sounds like fun," Lee said, taking up her writing paper and a pen.

Maggie turned and looked at her. Lee's face showed fatigue under its sensual beauty, but Maggie could see that her roommate was not so involved with herself as she was before.

"Hey, look," she said on impulse. "Shall we come back and get you? We can take you over to the club then."

"Thank you, Maggie, but I don't think so." Lee remembered her promise to Khai and didn't want to go out without her. "Some night I will—if I can bring a friend along."

"A guy? Why didn't you tell me?"

"No," Lee laughed, "It's the girl who works with me—Khai—"

"Oh," Maggie said in a bored voice, "Sure. If that's

what you want. Tomorrow some of the Green Berets are coming back to town. Why don't we do it then? Plan on it. Maybe you can question them about your dream lover."

Lee said, "I'll ask Khai and let you know tomorrow."

The bell rang for dinner and she carried her writing paper with her into the hall, leaving Maggie behind. Lee walked with her head held high, in spite of the wounded pride she felt. She cursed herself for having told Maggie her precious secret.

* * *

Khai asked Lee to join her in Saigon the following day and promised to go out with her and Maggie that night as well. It was their day off, but for the rest of the population it was an ordinary working day. People rose very early to set up fruit and flower stands in the streets. Lee and Khai went to town at ten and, on the way, Khai explained some of the architecture in her soft, careful voice.

"We do not have a battle with nature here," she said. "We do not build against the countryside, but we try to make our buildings harmonize with the trees and rocks. You will see."

And Lee did see. They went from Nguyen Hue Street, the scene of the City Hall riots, onto a riverside drive called Ben-Bach-Dang. Lee was astounded. Flowerbeds brilliant with colors after the monsoons grew thick along the pavement and flower vendors bobbed along beside them with huge bamboo baskets full of flowers. The women's *ao dais* added more color to the scene and the buildings were white and luxurious looking. Only the sight of planes overhead or army trucks and uniforms interfered with the gaiety of the city.

Khai brought Lee to a shop where both girls bought vividly colored silk and cotton for clothes. They browsed in other shops that contained embroidered goods, lacquers, and rattan furniture. They took their time until noon, when Khai suggested they buy some lunch and have a picnic in the botanical gardens. They walked down avenues arched by tamarinds that tried to shade the sidewalks from the boiling sun. When they entered a street where hoards of snack-venders were selling hot oriental cakes and sweets and sugar cane stalks, Lee bought a straw hat to protect her head from the heat. Fruit stands carried pineapples, oranges, bananas, papayas, and every other fruit that Lee could imagine. She let Khai choose the food for the picnic, and then they hailed a pedicab and were taken to the green botanical gardens.

Lee felt dizzy from the sun and the sight of all those brilliant colors, and she was very relieved when they sat down under cool trees beside a pond. There white ducks paddled in the water, a tempting sight, and orchids of all colors grew in voluminous patches. Khai took the lunch from the basket and set it out on the grass, explaining each cake to Lee.

"This is all incredible," Lee said in a soft voice.

"You must be tired. Usually we sleep from noon until two."

"That's a good idea. I can understand why."

"We will take a nap right here then," said Khai with a careless smile.

"No wonder you live in Saigon," said Lee, tasting the first sweet cake with pleasure. A papaya followed, moistening her tongue with its sweet juice.

"I knew you would like it," Khai said. "I came here for many reasons. My husband is away, for one."

"Your husband?" Lee asked in surprise.

"Yes. Pham. That is his name." Her eyes twinkled at the mention of his name, "But please don't speak of him to others. I'd rather be free of questions."

"I won't tell," said Lee. "But you must miss him."

"I miss him," said Khai.

She made it clear she didn't want to speak of him any more, so they gossiped about nurses, doctors, and patients they knew. Then both girls closed their eyes for a nap. Drowsily Lee wondered about Khai's husband and why he was such a mystery, but then she decided she knew nothing of life in this strange country and went to sleep.

When they woke, it was three o'clock and the sun was even hotter than before. Lee had to confess that she couldn't imagine doing any more sightseeing that day, and Khai agreed. They left the gardens and returned to the hospital, each one with a headache and a desire to be well by the evening.

Lee repressed any feelings of excitement she might have about getting out on the town that night. She merely thought of it as therapeutic, something she ought to do in order to feel more at ease in Saigon. In spite of her feeling of anger at Maggie, she herself wondered if she might find out more about Tom that night. She bathed and sat on her bed with her writing paper, but she couldn't concentrate.

Instead she daydreamed about Tom—the way he danced and held her in his arms. She resented his parents for believing he was dead, for they had accepted that as a fact months before. Her own parents too had accepted it and had argued with her before she left. But they didn't know how she felt, how she loved him. None of them knew him as a lover. None of them had planned for the future with him. Only she knew the part of him that would make a husband, and that was the part she owned and cherished.

When Maggie came in, she was still dreaming. But it was time to get dressed now, and Maggie was full of chatter about Bennie's trip to the Mekong Delta. She told Lee every detail about the battle waged there, while Lee thought of other things, her ears closed. Maggie wore a yellow chiffon dress this time, while Lee wore a slight black dress and a white lace stole.

"You look lovely, Doll," Maggie said, without looking at her.

Lee didn't care how she looked. She wore what she did only because Tom had loved the dress. It clung to her body gracefully and accented the swell of her breasts and the milky pallor of her skin. Her full lips and dark eyes needed no make-up. Nobody here would know that she had been a gawky, even ugly, child, that she had been

23

left out of friendships and games and dates for many years. Her daydreams had carried her through it, though the humiliation remained hidden inside her still. For years she had sat on the sidelines watching, never believing it when her mother said, "Your time will come." It was on the beautiful, graceful figure of Tom Lender that she had projected all her wishes for herself. But nobody here would ever know how Lee herself still thought of her face and body as laughable. She didn't believe the desires or flattery that had come her way.

She didn't even see the envy in Maggie's eyes when they left the room to meet Khai and Bennie in the hospital lobby.

Khai was dressed in a flowered silk *ao dai*, her sweet elfin face calm as she was introduced to Maggie and the plump, friendly Bennie.

They all went outdoors where the hot sky was cool and dark now, touched by sea breezes. A blue and yellow French Renault cab was waiting for them, and they drove through glittering boulevards to the officers' club.

"You'll get a kick out of this," said Bennie, as they climbed out of the cab. "The place is jam-packed. Lots of Green Berets for the gals."

"Anybody we know?" asked Maggie.

"Johnny Winston's there, with a group."

"Wow," whispered Maggie to Lee. "He's a great guy. Been wounded in action a couple of times and always goes right back. Last time he got shelled picking up two wounded tribesmen."

Bennie had reserved a table for them, and they sat down in the midst of whistles and stares from the crowds of officers of all ranks around them. Maggie was smiling happily and Khai's face was as calm and pleasant as ever. But Lee felt nervous, and she was glad when Bennie ordered a round of drinks for them. She didn't dare look around her, feeling that she would see people making fun of her or just plain ignoring her. Instead, she listened to Bennie talking to Khai in Vietnamese. He seemed to know it very well, and his face was serious under all the freckles, as was hers. Lee could understand only a few words of what they said, and it seemed to involve his recent mission in the Mekong Delta. In the background she could hear others discussing the war and the politics of Vietnam, and she was confused and upset by her own ignorance. She looked at Maggie for comfort, but her roommate was watching Bennie talk to Khai, her eyes two jealous slits.

All at once Bennie was on his feet, smiling again, and Khai and Maggie were looking up at a group of Green Berets standing beside their table. Lee's heart jumped to her throat at the sight of the uniforms that called up so many memories. She found herself staring into the blue eyes of one of them and being introduced to those same blue eyes.

"Lee, this is Johnny Winston," said Bennie, and then he introduced the other two men.

They pulled up chairs and Lee found herself next to Johnny. Nervously she glanced at him. His face was unusual—not conventionally handsome—for he looked both tired and tough at the same time. His lips had a slight, sarcastic smile while his eyes were warmly smiling. He sat very much at ease, his hard physique relaxed. She noted a scar on his upper lip and another on his left temple, and she looked down, where her drink was waiting.

"Drink up and relax," said Johnny. "You look scared."

She obeyed, for some reason relieved that he had noticed how scared she really was. He began to ask her questions: how long she had been in Saigon, how did she like it, what was her job. Lee answered as quickly as possible, then asked him where he had trained for the special forces and what year he had finished. He told her, and with a jolt, she realized he was only one year ahead of Tom. Now she didn't know what to do. She longed to ask him if he knew Tom, but didn't dare, in case he would say no.

"Did you know someone in my class?" he asked with a grin.

"Yes," she laughed.

"You're beautiful," he whispered, and then asked: "What's his name?"

At that point Maggie leaned forward and said in a brassy voice, "His name is Tom, and Lee here has come to find him. They're engaged, but she just won't believe that her boy friend is dead."

Everyone fell silent and looked at Lee, whose cheeks were flaming.

"Well now," Johnny said at last, in his easy, soft voice. "Maybe we can help her find out. I'll just take her on over to the corner for a quiet drink and we'll talk about it."

He stood up and reached out his hand to Lee, who took it, unable to say a word. She followed him through the crowds of staring men, her face lowered in embarrassment, near to tears of shame. Johnny led her to a table in a far corner, as he had promised, and quickly ordered them drinks. He leaned back in his chair again, changed from the fast-moving fighter to the easy listener.

"Come on now, kid. Stop looking so glum and tell me about it," he said.

She looked at him for signs of trust and honor and found them there.

CHAPTER 3

That night she talked to Johnny Winston for two hours; and much as she tried, she couldn't get him to tell her about himself. Later she thought that he was the strangest person she ever met—a hero with the face and manners of a poet. He didn't make fun of her search for Tom but seemed to understand what it meant to love somebody to that extent. Afterward she felt very relieved and couldn't get angry at Maggie who had been the cause for her confession to Johnny.

They went home at midnight. The air was sweet with the smell of damp flowers, and the cicadas were singing shrilly. Lee gazed out the window and wondered where Tom was, how long it would be before she saw him again. The chatter of Khai's and Maggie's voices passed right through her because she was so lost in her own dreams, and she was surprised when they reached the hospital so quickly. Bennie took them to the door.

"Thanks a lot," said Lee.

"Thank you, Ben," said Khai.

And they went into the bright lobby, leaving Maggie behind to say goodnight to Bennie. Inside, both girls paused, for there was a group of navy men and one civilian standing around a doctor.

"Must have been an accident," said Khai.

"Oh dear," whispered Lee.

She looked at Khai, who seemed very still beside her, and saw that she was staring at the tall, gray-haired man in the crowd; he was wearing a dark suede jacket and boots. Khai started to go, but the man detached himself from the group and came over to the girls.

"Khai," he said. *"Tu vas bien?"*

In English, Khai said, "I am fine. This is my friend Lee. Lee, this is Charles Marcel."

He shook Lee's hand but stared into Khai's face, his eyes demanding and melancholy. But Lee saw that Khai was avoiding his gaze by staring at the floor, and she didn't know whether to go or stay.

"What happened?" Khai asked the Frenchman in a soft voice.

"There was some trouble in the Vaico River—"

"Where in the Vaico?"

"A few miles south of my plantation, near your home . . . but it was all on the water. The U.S. was navigating a new kind of ship there and the Viet Cong exploded it. That is all."

"What part did you play in this, Charles?" she asked, now looking at him directly.

His gaze didn't waver from hers. "I saw the explosion and took my truck down. I brought the wounded here."

"All Americans?"

"Three Annamites."

Khai turned and walked away, her face down, and Lee started to follow. But Charles Marcel stopped her with a light touch on her arm.

"Won't you sit down for a minute?" he inquired, and he smiled, his face a mass of lines. "I'd like to talk to somebody while I smoke a cigarette."

Lee said, "All right," and followed him to a white vinyl couch along the cement wall farthest from the group of navy men. She went with him, partly because her faith in people had been restored by Johnny and partly because she wanted him to explain a little of the war to her, if he could. She had seen that Khai was avoiding him not from dislike but from some other obscure reason.

"You are a friend of Khai's then?" he asked, when they were seated.

"Yes, but I just arrived recently."

"She is worried about her family, of course. It seems the Viet Cong are in that area—which is also my area. I am now planning to sell my plantation—rubber—to the

Americans. I'm tired of the troubles." He tried to relax by leaning back, but Lee could see that he was very nervous. His fingers trembled around his cigarette. "My wife too. She is tired of them . . . How is Khai?"

"She seems happy to me," said Lee, not sure what she should and shouldn't tell this man. "How do you know her?"

"She is my half-sister. My father impregnated her mother twenty-three years ago." He sighed and then smiled at Lee. "I suppose all the problems here confuse you. In every Vietnamese face on the street, you will find the life of an idea. Each person represents a purpose, and each person is a victim of contradictory experiences. I don't know what idea Khai represents, since she is especially discreet. I only know how she is a victim."

The most Lee knew came from the books of Dr. Tom Dooley, and she remembered now his descriptions of the refugees from North Vietnam, their illness and confusion. But that was a long time ago, and nothing was settled yet.

"Do you think the Americans will help win the war?" she asked.

"If there is a victory, they will have helped. If there isn't, they will have helped again." He shrugged, inhaling on his cigarette, and looked at Lee curiously, "Do you think that is a silly thing to say?"

"I don't know," said Lee. "I was brought up to believe in my country, right or wrong . . ."

"And now you find that there is no such thing as right or wrong?"

"I find that it's hard to know."

"Well, your job is to clean up after them, and that is invaluable. For a woman, peace is the only true way of life, don't you think?"

"Yes. I hate to see women suffering in this war."

"Khai too. She suffers, but I hope to God she is not involved. Peace of mind should be her lot." He put out his cigarette and gave Lee a long, questioning look, and then he said, "Would you like to come out to visit my wife and me one day? Come along with a friend, who can show you the way. You should see some more of the countryside. It is quite pretty. Under Diem our plantation flourished again, but now it is hopeless. We like having visitors, I can assure you, so please feel welcome."

He wrote down his name and address on a slip of paper and handed it to Lee. She was pleased and impressed by this man who seemed both sympathetic and intelligent, and she promised him she would try to visit him soon. He rose and returned to the group of navy men, while she went on to her room.

She found Maggie there, unclipping her earrings in front of the mirror, her lipstick smeared and her gestures uncertain. Lee said hello and thanked Maggie for the evening, but she got no reply. So she began to undress, her heart still uplifted by the meeting with Johnny and now by the meeting with Charles Marcel. She went to wash herself and when she returned she found Maggie sitting on the edge of the bed, still fully dressed.

"You're very lucky to have someone as nice as Bennie," Lee said in the way of a compliment.

"You mean, enjoy it while you can, Maggie ol' gal—right?"

"No. I meant that I like him. That's all," said Lee and she removed her slip self-consciously.

"Just because of your body, you get what you want," Maggie said, staring at Lee, "36–24–36 and you've got it made. Still, little Lee has to go around playing the part of Miss Faithful all day long. It makes her look chaste . . . you and Khai, the two good girls with beautiful bodies and faces to top it off. Teases. Both of you are teases."

Lee didn't answer, but climbed into her nightgown, with her face averted. Her knees felt weak, her head dizzy, as Maggie spoke.

"Now you're going to bed for your beauty rest after teasing Johnny Winston all night and, for a li'l nightcap that aging Frenchie downstairs . . . I know your kind . . . you and Khai."

Lee got into bed and turned her face to the wall.

"Khai—she's no sweet little lotus girl. You just wait

and see, Doll. I'll turn over her rug and show the dirt. It's always there somewhere."

Lee sat up, livid with anger now, and looked at Maggie's pasty, ragged face. "Why do you have to make everything vulgar?" Lee asked her. "Can't you leave anything alone?"

"Me? Vulgar!" Maggie cried, "I'll show you who's vulgar."

She stood up in a threatening way but sat down again, her legs too unsteady to carry her. Lee lay down again, wondering what Maggie had planned on doing. She was sickened by her and sorry for her too. She turned off her bedside light and closed her eyes, unwilling and unable to continue the fight. But it went on in her mind, until she began to wonder if Maggie didn't have a point.

Was she a tease in fact? In a way, she was, she realized; but then Maggie didn't know how much she hated herself and how little faith she had in her appearance. She remembered Johnny whispering "You're beautiful" and it reminded her of Tom saying the same to her one day. The spontaneous way Johnny said it made her believe for a minute it was true. Why did she refuse to accept herself as a grown woman, she wondered?

She knew one thing. Seeing Maggie so dishevelled and plain made her sick, as if Maggie were a mirror for herself. For Lee really did see herself as an awkward, homely girl. When she first went into nursing, it was partly because she identified with sick and lonely people. She wanted to help them get better, stronger, so they could return to their lives as full people. All that time she carried around a picture of Tom, as if his graceful, athletic body and handsome face could cure her.

Lee opened her eyes and looked at Maggie struggling out of her yellow dress. It was true that Maggie made everything around her vulgar and that she would lose what she most wanted—Bennie—because of it. Lee wanted to tell her that but didn't dare. It would only make Maggie a more dangerous enemy against Khai. Lee closed her eyes again . . . and slept this time.

31

The next morning Lee was in the operating room without a break. Several soldiers had been very badly wounded. Two of them would have legs amputated; another had a severe brain injury; another was blind. It was the first time Lee had come in contact with the severely disabled, and, while she helped Dr. Curtis apply temporary treatment, her mind fought against anguish. It wouldn't do any good to lose control of her emotions while these poor, mutilated men were requiring the most efficient care. Their faces were unmarked by age, only by injury. They lay unconscious under the bright lights of the operating room, unaware of the damage that had been done, the adjustments they would have to make in the months to come.

At noon Lee's shift arrived and she had to leave for the *Charity*. She could take her lunch break at the hospital when she wanted, but this day she didn't feel like eating. The official car was waiting to drive her to the ship and she climbed into the back seat to sit beside an open window. Two other nurses accompanied her over, but Lee didn't have the heart to talk to them.

It was a very hot day and the sun made the sky white, so that the small clouds were almost invisible against the glare. In Saigon the white buildings had sharp shadows on their walls and the flowers were especially bright. The streets were quiet at this hour and the car moved quickly through the small traffic of bicycles and pedicabs. Lee stared outside without seeing a thing.

The morning's work stayed with her, like a bad dream. She couldn't detach herself from the men she had seen. They seemed very innocent against the chaos of the war. She remembered a line from one of Tom's letters that went: "The bravery of our men seems automatic, in spite of all the training. I saw one die in the field a couple of days ago. I held him against me and cried for the first time in many years. He was a friend of mine."

"If only I could find him!" her mind cried out again.

But there was always more work to be done, to distract her from her thoughts about him. And now it was teaching. The car stopped at the end of the dock and she climbed out with the other two nurses. The *Charity* was anchored in the middle of the port now and they had to go out on a small tug. Lee stood at the railing while gulls flew around looking for fish and junks slipped by through the oily waters, their hulls weighted down with cargo. The water was of a muddy color and the heat was almost unbearable as it reflected off the surface of the water.

On the *Charity* coffee and sandwiches were set out in the dining room and Lee managed to eat before her class. A group of thirty men and women were waiting for her, and a slide projector had been set up ahead of time, so she could get to work immediately. This day she was showing pictures of people suffering from the various tropical fungus infections, as well as diseases caused by micro-organisms.

The pictures were horrifying and drew gasps from the audience. Lee, who had seen them a week before, was sickened by them this time herself. She would stand beside the projected image of a child deformed by a fungus infection and describe the treatment in as cool a voice as she could manage. She would raise the sample vial of penicillin to a small beam of light and puncture the lid with the sample needle, showing exactly how much should be administered to the patient each time.

Most days she would describe how to set up a dispensary and how to keep a village clean—by digging deeper wells, boiling the drinking water, and such. She had to describe how to deliver a baby too. It was interesting to her to hear the reactions of her Vietnamese students to her lessons, and they often had stories to tell about illnesses and sanitary conditions in the towns they came from.

But this day's class was upsetting to everyone, including Lee. The contrast between her own life and that of the peasants was so great that she felt her own problems receding into proportion.

After her class, a slim Vietnamese girl approached Lee at the desk. Her shy smile was vaguely familiar and Lee realized she must be Khai's sister.

"I want to ask a question," the girl said in a soft, hesitating voice.

"Yes?"

"When do we learn how to treat the wounded people?"

"Very soon," said Lee. "Next week we start that, and we will start taking patients onto the ship."

"I see. That is good."

And the girl slipped away before Lee could ask her if she were Khai's sister. Lee went on deck to wait for her next class, for she taught the same lesson twice a day. She stood at the railing under the hot sun and stared at the coastline before her. She realized she had seen very little of the country, and she wished she could follow Charles Marcel's offer to visit his plantation. But she would have no way of getting there.

"Nurse Knight," said a high voice, interrupting her thoughts.

Lee turned and saw the ship's head nurse beside her.

"I want to congratulate you on your teaching," said the woman. "You have been a great inspiration for your students, and most of them have already volunteered to work here on the boat when we go inland."

"When will you do that?" asked Lee.

"In two weeks. After your classes are done . . . It's a new plan," she said, "The government wants a roving medical ship. We would ask you to join us, but I gather you are too useful at the hospital."

The older woman gave Lee a quick, appraising look, and then she nodded and walked away. Lee watched her go and a feeling of pride came over her. It hadn't occurred to her that her superiors would be judging her actions, so she hadn't expected praise. To be useful was a surprisingly pleasant experience. In her years of training she had performed useful duties, but always offhandedly, for her mind was fixed on Tom at all times. All the lectures on what a fine thing it was to be a nurse—especially a navy nurse!—had passed over her head. She was doing it for personal reasons.

But now, looking across the water to Saigon, far away from home, she was proud to be useful. The wounded men she had seen that morning were not dream figures; they were very real. Lee remembered each one of them vividly and walked down to her second class with a feeling of pride that was strange to her.

Afterward, driving back to the hospital, she talked with the other girls in the car. The one named Nancy was very excited because one of the hospital corpsmen had asked her out on a date.

"I just love it here," she kept saying.

Her friend Carol asked Lee how she liked it.

"I'm just beginning to feel at home," Lee said.

"Me too," said Carol, who had a long, serious face. "I run a ward, and today we took in some Vietnamese. It's the first time I ever treated one. They're okay. But I still don't trust them."

"I suppose we have to trust them," said Lee, "if we want to take good care of them."

"Sure thing," said Carol, "but this war gives me the creeps. How do we know we won't be bombed on the street, or the ship, or even at the hospital. It gives me the creeps."

"I just love it here," Nancy said.

Lee had never thought of the possibility of being bombed on the street and she put the idea out of her mind at once. She knew such fears were dangerous, even if there was a grain of truth in them. "There is nothing to fear but fear itself," went through her mind, and she clung to it. The men on the field had a right to such fear, but even they put it aside when the chips were down.

She had other things to fear, she realized. Like Maggie. What kind of "dirt" was she going to get out of Khai's life? Lee thought she ought to speak with her roommate frankly, but she was afraid of causing more trouble between them. She returned to her room reluctantly, hoping

35

that Maggie would not be there. She wanted a quiet night for writing home and sleeping early.

When she arrived, the room was empty, and Lee removed her cloak and shoes at once. She considered taking a swim out in the hospital pool, a thing she had never done before, but she was shy of appearing in a bathing suit. Instead she took a cold shower and washed her hair.

Just as she returned to her room, the buzzer rang on her wall indicating that she had a phone call. Her first reaction was alarm, and then she thought it might be Maggie wanting something. She went down the hall to the phone booth, and said hello with a voice full of doubt.

"Hi there, kid," said Johnny Winston at the other end.

Lee's heart jumped, to her own surprise. He said she sounded as scared as ever and laughed warmly into the receiver.

"I didn't know who would be calling," Lee said with a smile.

"No wonder. You must get a lot of them."

"You're the first," she told him.

"Well! I'm glad I'm the first at something for you," he said. "How about dinner tonight?"

"I don't know—I planned to write letters—"

"Bring them along. You can write letters while I draw your picture."

"Well—okay," she said.

"I'll be by at seven, okay?"

She agreed to that and went back to her room, smiling. Maggie was there when she came in; she didn't look at Lee.

"Hi," said Lee. No answer. She sat on the bed to do her nails and smiled at the diamond ring on her finger as if it were her only friend.

CHAPTER 4

Lee wore a cool white linen dress that night and pearl earrings Tom had given her for her birthday. Johnny was in civilian clothes, so she hardly recognized him. He met her in the lobby of the hotel and they took a cab to the French quarter of Saigon, where a small restaurant with an outdoor section was hidden among small buildings. The night was so warm that they sat outside. Johnny ordered a bottle of wine and they both had *boeuf bourguignon* to eat.

"I feel strange—eating so well when nearby people are starving," said Lee.

"It's hard," he agreed, and poured them each a glass of wine, his eyes on Lee's face. "You look thoughtful tonight."

"I'm just beginning to feel involved with my patients —that's all," Lee murmured, and then smiled at him, "But tonight I want to hear about you—how you came to be a hero."

"Well, let me see," said Johnny with a grin. "The first thing I did was run gallantly out onto the field to pick up a wounded body and run back again . . . It turned out to be a Viet Cong. I didn't know what to do. So I hid him in a bush and ran out to pick up two of our tribesmen—just to make things even—and when I got back, everyone said I was wonderful."

Lee laughed and said she didn't believe it. But he promised her it was true. She looked at him with interest, for his face was so lively it attracted attention and still he had an underlying quietude. The way he used his hands,

37

she thought, he was the last person to be involved in hand-to-hand guerrilla combat.

"What's your occupation in the special forces?" she asked him.

"Medic," he said.

That made sense, she thought, and asked him: "Why did you enlist?"

"I didn't have anything else I wanted to do at the time. I did badly in school, so I couldn't go on with football or wrestling," he said with his sarcastic smile, "and I wanted to be an athlete. So I enlisted. While I was in boot camp I decided to take a few years to perfect some skills—and here I am."

"What do you think about the war?" she asked him.

"I don't," he replied. "It's too confused for anyone's brain. I just perform my duties."

"Why do—?"

"Uh uh," he interrupted, shaking his head, "No more questions from you, kid."

She smiled and obeyed, while he watched her closely.

"You know, I remember your boy friend," Johnny said all at once, "I saw him around in Georgia and then again out here. A good-looking boy with lots of guts."

Lee stared at him in amazement. The fact that he had seen Tom astounded her and brought him immediately to mind again.

"Why didn't you tell me last night?" she asked.

"I didn't want to. You were too upset . . . Besides, there isn't much for me to say. I might have said two words to him before I heard that he was—had disappeared —and that was that." Johnny shrugged and poured each of them more wine, "I asked around after you left last night. Nobody knew him very well. Said he stuck to himself a lot. I guess he had you on his mind. One of the guys in there who saw you last night said Tom had a picture of you he showed around."

Lee looked at a group of soldiers passing on the street and her eyes glistened with tears. There was a time she sat on a sidewalk cafe in New York with Tom, just like this, when they had discussed the travelling they would do after he had served in Vietnam. Where was he now? How far she had come to find him! It seemed it got harder, the closer she got. She tried to control the tears that grew in her eyes by counting the passing soldiers, but it didn't do any good until Johnny nudged her.

He pointed at a group of three Vietnamese girls trailing the soldiers; they wore short skirts, American style, and lots of lipstick.

"Guess what they want," he whispered.

Lee smiled and said, "You'd be happier now with one of them . . . I'm a mess."

"I know you are," he agreed and leaned back in his chair. "But I don't want to exploit the war through them. I'll do it through you instead."

"How?"

"You wouldn't be here if there weren't a war. And I like looking at you."

Johnny looked her over, making her blush, and she remembered what Maggie had said about being a tease. She felt awkward as he watched her in her white dress that held close to her bosom and thighs, and she leaned forward, hiding herself.

At that moment there was some commotion and shouting on the street; they stood up to see what was happening. The three girls that had passed were in the middle of a group of soldiers, half of them American, half of them Vietnamese; the latter were trying to drag them away while the Americans held on tight to the girls' arms.

"There's war for you," Johnny said to Lee.

It began to turn into a fight between the soldiers, and the girls were shoved brutally aside as the men attacked each other, all of them armed. A waiter came out of the restaurant and joined Lee and Johnny.

"*Vive la guerre*," he said.

"Which one?" Johnny asked and said, "Go call the police," to the waiter in French.

The waiter scurried inside at once, knocking over a glass of wine as he went. Meanwhile, the shouts were getting louder and passers-by, most of them in uniform, were stopping to join in or watch. The girls were standing close together crying and talking to each other. It was obvious they wanted to get away, but now a group of Vietnamese men held them where they stood.

"It's against the law," Johnny said.

Lee was shaken by the sight of the violence and held onto a post supporting the restaurant awning. All at once she found herself alone and saw Johnny going out onto the street to join the mob. He disappeared and the cries and shouts of the crowd grew louder in the night air. The waiter returned and stood beside Lee.

"The cops are coming," he said in French and shook his head sadly.

Lee stared into the crowd, seeking Johnny, and she heard the cries growing lower and the voices diffusing into talk. The crowd began to move toward the girls then and they cowered closer together. Lee felt sorry for them, they were so frightened. A siren began to whine in the distance, and faces turned around with looks of alarm. Lee caught a glimpse of Johnny under a streetlight, talking to the men who held the girls, and everyone was turning in the direction of the siren's whine.

Finally Johnny pushed the girls into a doorway, and they disappeared inside, and the crowd dispersed—either running or walking at a forced saunter. The siren grew closer now. Lee's heart was in her throat, as she watched Johnny amble across the street, very much at ease, and return to the restaurant. The waiter muttered his relief in French and ran inside, just as the police van came around the corner, lights flashing.

"Now sit down and have some wine," said Johnny.

Her legs weak, she sat back in her seat and handed Johnny her glass of wine. His lay shattered on the tiled floor. They sat in silence, as the police van drove slowly along, only once stopping to question one of the passing soldiers. Then it turned a corner and disappeared.

"I tell you," Johnny said, "it's just not safe to exploit the war through those girls. Their men don't like it."

"So that was it," said Lee.

"The girls like it all right, for awhile, but things are

not what they seem to be here. Under every smile there lies a plan for death—on both sides." He sighed quickly, then closed his eyes and listened to the cicadas chirping.

Lee looked at him with admiration. His face, though scarred, was strong. His sarcasm concealed the ability to act with love. There was something very lonely about him, and she wondered if all the Green Berets had that quality of aloneness, if that was the essence of heroism. For the first time, she wondered if he were married. He turned his head and smiled at her.

"Let's go," he said.

He paid the bill and she followed him out onto the now empty street. He took her arm and they walked down several quiet, tree-lined streets in silence. Tall palms lined Le Loi Boulevard, where the wide sidewalks were almost empty. The clop-clop of horses' footsteps emerged from the silence and a rustic pony trap passed by, driven by two straw-hatted people from the country. Their wagon was empty after a day of vending.

Johnny stopped a pedicab and helped Lee inside, without saying a word. He followed her in and directed the driver to the hospital. The wheels creaked under them, and Lee glanced at Johnny, wondering at his mood. He looked very quiet and content enough, but she was afraid she would never see him again and it worried her.

The quiet streets passed by and neither of them spoke, until the hospital showed beyond some trees. Then Johnny took Lee's left hand and lifted the ring finger up to see the diamond.

"I never gave a girl a ring," he said, answering the question that had begun to haunt her, "but if I did, it would have to be like this one."

"Thank you," Lee said.

"And the girl would have to be like you," Johnny said with a smile at her. "How's that for praise?"

"Fair," she smiled.

But she shivered inside, taken with a sudden fear that made her recoil inside herself. She could speak smoothly, but her blood was racing with a new kind of fear she couldn't understand.

41

They stopped outside the hospital and Johnny walked her to the door.

"Well, Lee," he said, "I'll find out what I can about Tom. Tomorrow I'm going to the Cambodian border. I'll call you when I get back."

"Good," she whispered. "Thank you for tonight."

"Thank you," he said and walked away.

She didn't watch him go, but went inside. Her confusion was mixed with gladness that he would call her when (and if!) he returned, and she didn't dare ask herself why she was confused.

* * *

Although she was working very hard the next few days, Lee always had time to get reports from the Cambodian border, where battles were being fought relentlessly. She would treat the wounded and get information from Khai or Maggie about the course the war was taking. The situation was uneasy even in Saigon, where changes in the government were expected but not desired by the Americans. Occasional riots would be suppressed by the military police in the city and the suppression would result in cries about police brutality.

Each morning Lee feared finding Johnny on the operating table and she would check the list of patients who came in during the night. Each night she sat in her room or went to the library, hoping to avoid Maggie. Her noon lunch hour would be spent with Khai, who was especially quiet these days but always pleasant and trustworthy. Lee told her about Johnny and the riot over the street girls, and Khai smiled and said, "It is to be expected." But Lee never asked Khai any questions, respecting the girl's silence when it came to herself.

However, this silence had to be broken at last. One night Maggie slammed into their room at midnight, her blond curls messy and her lipstick smeared. She had been out with Bennie and looked unusually sober. Lee looked up from her desk, where she was writing a letter to a friend at home.

"Well, Miss Faithful," said Maggie. "Now I know the dirt about your friend Khai. I overheard her talking to one of my wards—a little Vietnamese man—and it looks as if he's a Victor Charlie and so is she!" Maggie tossed her coat on the bed and put her hands on her hips, confronting Lee with short breath. "So you see. She's not a sweet little thing after all. You and Bennie are blind wrong."

"What has Bennie got to do with it?" Lee asked as calmly as she could.

"He's got a very high opinion of her—that's what."

"She's an intelligent girl," Lee said.

"Ha! As if that's what he likes about her, Miss Faithful. No sir. Right now he's talking to her down in the lobby. She just happened to be passing through. The little whore."

Lee stood up and faced Maggie fully. "Don't talk like that," she said. "You're doing yourself more damage than anyone else."

"Oh, I am, am I? Well, in that case, I'll just have to get efficient about the whole thing. I already reported Victor Charlie downstairs. He was pulled out of the Vaicon River, with all his VC medals gone. He came in with your charming Frenchman that night. So there—you see? I'm not kidding."

Lee sat down again, taken aback. What if Charles Marcel—Khai's own half-brother!—had brought in the Viet Cong as part of a whole plan? She didn't know anything about the intrigue in this war, so she had to operate on faith alone. She didn't know what to say to Maggie, who knew more about the city and the war than she.

"Have you reported Khai?" she asked at last.

"No, not yet," Maggie replied, going to the mirror to cream her face.

"Why not?"

"I'm a nurse, not a spy. I don't want to get the wrong reputation."

"But you must be proud of finding the enemy by accident?"

Maggie glanced at Lee and her face showed some nervousness. She said, "Somebody else should report Khai."

"Who, for instance?" Lee asked.

"You."

"I wasn't there, and how do I know that Khai is involved?"

"She was talking to him about an attack on some town where her family lives. Isn't that enough? The man is a commie."

"What will you do if I don't report Khai?"

"I'll report you and Khai," said Maggie, "It's part of your job as an ensign in the navy."

"This is turning into a joke," said Lee, and she smiled in spite of her fear. "I wasn't even there, Maggie. How can I report it?"

"Get the truth out of her yourself, and take it from there. Use your noggin, Miss Faithful. You may be here for romantic reasons, but the rest of us are fighting a war against the Communists. Even little lotus blossom is fighting a war."

"If Khai is involved, she obviously won't tell me."

"If you're smart, you can get it out of her. Maybe you're not smart."

"That isn't the point, is it?" Lee said. "Whether I'm smart or not. The point is, I don't really want to be involved in this."

"What are you doing in the navy?" Maggie demanded, her face a white blob of cream.

Lee fell silent. Maggie always hit one nail on the head in her giant assaults. It was true that her duty as an ensign should be to her country, although she normally thought of herself as a nurse first. And now a real friendship was involved, for Lee considered Khai a friend. She didn't know what to say to Maggie, who was obviously avoiding reporting Khai herself for the most personal reasons. Bennie would resent her for her suspicions, if they turned out to be wrong, and maybe even if they turned out to be right. Lee could see Maggie's point about the war, however, and she was involved in it as a member of the navy.

"All right," she said at last, "I'll talk to Khai and try to find out what I can and then I'll decide what to do, if it's true what you think. But from now on, the decisions are mine, Maggie. You've handed them over."

"What do you mean by that?" Maggie asked.

"I mean, whatever information I get is mine alone, and I choose what to do with it."

"You're smarter than I thought, after all," Maggie said. "Too bad you're all tied up in a dream . . . I hear you went out with Johnny Winston the other night. Where does that put your long lost love?"

"I don't want to talk about it, Maggie," said Lee.

"We sure make a happy couple in our little room thirty-seven, don't we? It's something to write home about."

"I'm sorry it's turning out this way. It doesn't make things easier for either of us."

"No, it doesn't. Maybe you want to get a transfer?"

Lee looked at Maggie and saw beneath all the cream and mascara that her expression showed pain, as if her feelings were hurt. Lee tried to understand, even sympathize, but she couldn't. Maggie had done so much damage that it was up to her to make the efforts toward friendship again. Maggie left their room now to wash, and Lee removed her dressing gown and climbed into bed. It was always a relief to lie down after the day's work, but this night sleep did not come easily for her.

She was worried about Khai and how to go about approaching her, and she also found herself worrying about Johnny. He had been gone several days and the reports on the wars were blood-filled. Of course she hoped that he would bring news of Tom, but especially that he would come back in one piece. Lee tried to conjure up Tom's face, to see it in detail, but it was clouded by time, and she thought of getting up to look at his photograph. But Maggie came into the room, and Lee turned her face to the wall.

For some reason, with her eyes closed she remembered the last line of Tom's last letter to her: "If none of our plans come off, make it with somebody else, my darling, and that way the dream will last." It made tears sting her eyes, as she lay there alone in bed in the strange city of Saigon. What was she doing there? Would she ever see his face again? She wanted to know the truth now and only the truth. More than ever. If she never saw him again, what would she do? How could she make the dream last? She didn't know. The only thing she heard before going to sleep was the roar of military planes overhead, and they led her into dreams of fighting on distant hills near Cambodia.

CHAPTER 5

The following morning was calm in the operating room, but there were reports of more men to come before the day was over. The mission in Cambodia was finished for awhile, and it was considered successful in spite of the many American casualties. In the operating room the nurses performed a few menial duties, while Dr. Curtis sat with them, sipping coffee.

"Okay," he said, after a while. "Let's go out for a quick swim."

Lee was surprised and glanced out the window where the warm sun sparkled on the turquoise pool. She could see no people out there, lounging or swimming now, and so she agreed to go.

She went upstairs and changed into her polka-dot two-piece suit, tied her hair in a bandana, and joined the others on the hot cement around the pool. Khai wore a modest bathing suit the mustard color of the sails on junks, and she waved Lee over to a chair beside her. Dr. Curtis, on the edge of the pool, stopped Lee as she was passing him.

"We may need your help later tonight," he said, "The Australian girl, Betsy, has caught something—"

"Serious?" Lee asked with concern.

"No, I don't think so. But we're always on guard. That malaria they can't cure is getting some of the boys . . . Anyway, come down after dinner. That should do it," he said and plunged headlong into the water.

Lee put on her sunglasses and joined Khai. She was worried by the doctor's remark. She knew very little of this new kind of malaria, only that a couple of men had

47

been sent home with it, and that the regular cure wasn't working. If there were an epidemic, it could be disastrous. Although the Vietnamese were burdened by many diseases, they were also immune to others that a foreigner could pick up quickly.

"Is something wrong?" Khai inquired, scrutinizing Lee's face.

"No—not really," Lee said and smiled at her friend.

Now it struck her that this was a ripe moment to begin her questioning of Khai, but the whole idea repelled her. In her bathing suit, Khai looked like a child and her round face, though sensual, seemed innocent. Lee trusted her and hated the task she had been given by Maggie. . . How could she begin? She closed her eyes and listened to the splashing of Dr. Curtis in the pool; the water sounded very inviting.

"Did you ever learn to swim?" she asked Khai.

"Not well. My brother used to throw me into the river and I would flop around, very scared."

"I don't blame you. What they call 'horsing around' at home used to scare me to death."

Khai laughed. " 'Horsing around'—very descriptive," she said and added, "Anything violent upsets me quite a bit."

"Me too." Lee glanced at Khai quickly, "But you must have seen a lot of it."

"I have," said Khai, "but I am not used to it yet."

"Does your husband come from the same hamlet as you?" Lee ventured.

"No. From far away north. From Hue, the old Imperial Capital of Vietnam. It is on the banks of the River of Perfumes. A beautiful, sad place, where the tombs of emperors are hidden away in vegetation." Khai smiled in a distant way and said, "Pham has a poem about it: the murmur of pines, the dipping of oars and the soft flight of birds. I was never there myself, but he has told me of it."

"Where did you meet him?"

"At the University here in Saigon," said Khai, and her face became closed and serious.

Lee didn't know what to say. She felt it was unfair to

48

continue her prying in this way. She was using the tactics of military spying, she thought, when the just and humane way to question a friend was direct. She stared at the blue and silver glitter of water, at Dr. Curtis's arms doing the crawl up and down the length of the pool. Her heart pounded nervously at the prospect of direct inquiry.

"Did Charles tell you about me?" Khai asked all at once.

"He told me you're his half-sister."

"He always has to tell. You would think he was proud of it." And she gave a harsh laugh that was unlike her, "So. You know I have French blood."

"Yes. Is that bad?"

"For me, yes. I am Vietnamese first."

"Is blood important in this war?" Lee asked.

"Very. But isn't it always? You have your ethnic groups at war in America. We have Cham and Annamite. Not only that, we have the intrusion of many others—Japanese, Chinese, French . . . We do not mean to become a melting pot, as you call it. We mean to be what we are at heart—Vietnamese. That is all."

"Did you know that Maggie reported a Viet Cong patient yesterday?"

"Yes. I know that."

Khai and Lee looked at each other from behind their dark glasses, their eyes serious.

"Why do you ask?" Khai inquired.

"She suspects you of the same thing. But she wanted me to find out."

Khai smiled all at once and leaned out to squeeze Lee's hand.

"Dear Lee," she said, "go for a swim and let me think how to answer you."

Relieved, Lee removed her sunglasses and tucked her hair into her bathing cap. The cement was baking under her feet and the sparkling water had the appeal of a mirage. She dove straight into the cool water and headed down to the bottom where she trailed her fingers along the cement. Then she crawled her way up again, squint-

49

ing at the prismic surface from underneath. She reached air beside Dr. Curtis, who splashed water in her face with his hand and continued his trip down to the other end of the pool. Lee laughed and did another nose dive to the base of the pool again. She had forgotten what a simple pleasure could be, how purifying it was to swim and enjoy herself. When she came up again, Dr. Curtis was floating on his back.

Lee began to swim the length of the pool again, catching glimpses of Khai lost in thought on the sidelines. As she swam, she felt the tropical sun on her face, burning her; she saw a jay flying over the hospital, snipping the air with its wings. All problems seemed as elusive as the jay flying into the distance, and Lee swam her way into complete relaxation before returning to Khai. Dr. Curtis was still floating blissfully, his face to the sun, when Lee climbed out of the pool.

Khai handed her a towel, but it was unnecessary when the sun was so hot, and Lee released her hair and flopped down beside Khai.

"It's lovely," she said, "Shall I teach you to swim one day?"

"Oh yes!" Khai exclaimed.

"I don't want to get too brown, or red," Lee said and pushed her chair into some shade, where she could still see Khai and read the expression in her face.

"If you visit Charles, you will be seeing the country near my home," Khai said in a soft voice, "and perhaps he will take you to our pagoda. We are very proud of it."

"I hope I can see it. Do you visit Charles ever?"

"No, I do not. We run into each other from time to time, and that is quite enough . . . Both my brother and my father died of beri-beri, you see, and they were very sick when my mother went to old Marcel for help. He gave her help, so that my other brothers and sisters were all right, and he gave her me as well. And Khoung."

"Where is your mother now?"

"At home."

"Do you ever visit her?"

"As much as I can," said Khai. "But then I only tell

you this to show you how I am . . . Pham is different. Maybe only because he is a man. I don't know the answer to that. He fights with his body, not just with his mind, and I know many of his friends, like the man that Maggie discovered. This is what we call *chien tranh nhan*, the people's war. Naturally we know one another, we people.

"But I feel as you do, Lee, when it comes to war. It is no solution and the terrible wounds we see are a waste. I feel the pain of an American soldier, just as I do of a Vietnamese. It is all foolish, and worse than foolish . . . I have no political affiliations, as they say. I want to see my husband well and proud, and my family too."

Khai's face revealed pain as she said this, as if she doubted the possibility of her family being saved. She squeezed her hands together in her lap and frowned behind her sunglasses.

"I share my husband's bitterness, but not his masculine pride. That is all."

Lee sighed to herself, understanding the dreadful pain her friend must feel. She felt ashamed that she had had a moment's doubt about Khai, who was so gentle with the patients and so sympathetic as a friend. But even more than that, she was afraid for Khai and all women, including herself, whose men were fighters.

The blue sky and the tall mahogany trees contained many secrets, Lee thought, and she remembered the nurse in the car saying how bombs might drop out of nowhere. The shifting sun moved along the roof of the hospital and cast a shadow on the pool. Lee stared at it and then at Khai, who sat in a position of surrender to the heat of the day.

* * *

After dinner Lee went into the nurse's station to wash and change into her uniform. There were two other girls there, and she listened to their conversation before a full-length mirror, where they were reflected, two redheads in white.

"It's a tragedy," one of them said.

"You're not kidding . . . I just hope I don't catch it. You never know."

"No, you never do."

"As if it wasn't bad enough getting shot to bits."

"Malaria is something else. If they don't find a cure fast, we'll lose this war for sure."

"It makes me wonder whose side God is on."

"Me too."

And they left Lee alone in the station. She pinned her cap on before the empty mirror, wondering what the conversation was all about. If Betsy, the girl she was replacing, had caught malaria, an epidemic could begin within the hospital; that would be a disaster. If the soldiers were getting it now, it was just as bad. Many medical men were working in the field of preventative disease at home, she knew, and that was not her area. She had to concentrate her concern on the wounded and avoid panic about catching diseases.

The last group of casualties and wounded from the Cambodian border came in that night. They arrived at the hospital by means of a helicopter that landed on the playing field outside; the bodies were carried in litters, and they awaited treatment in the out-patient emergency section of the hospital. Often friends accompanied them from the field and stayed with them before their treatment was determined.

As Lee passed the line of wounded men on her way to the operating room, she received a few whistles and outstretched hands, and she tried to maintain a balance between a warm response to these men and the coolness that her uniform required. But she was appalled by the people she saw, their faces and bodies wrapped in temporary bandages that didn't conceal the blood, some of them stretched out silently, covered by a blanket, some of them covered completely, their faces removed from the world forever.

She felt a hand on her shoulder and turned with a half-smile. There was Johnny, his green beret tipped to one side, his smile as sarcastic as ever, his face and body free of wounds. Lee started to hug him with pleasure, she was so glad to see him, but she withheld herself.

"Hi, kid," he said.

"You're all right . . . I'm so glad."

"On duty tonight?"

Lee nodded.

"How about tomorrow?"

"I don't know," she admitted. "The regular girl is sick. I might have to replace her."

"I'll call you, then," he said.

She saw a young boy sitting nearby, watching them, and he looked at Johnny with adoring eyes. His soft features, almost too young for a beard, were bandaged on the left side, and his expression showed the effects of morphine. She looked at Johnny again.

"Please do call me," she said. "I have to run."

He nodded and patted her arm, and as she started away, the young boy said to her.

"Love him, lady . . . He's a great man."

And the bandaged Negro face beside the boy nodded wearily and added, "Johnny saved the kid's life . . . Nurse, I need help."

Her eyes filled and Lee said, "As fast as possible."

She hurried on down to the operating room, feeling great anguish for these people and only too eager to start treatment. She washed her hands, slipped on her mask, and went in to replace the other nurse and join Dr. Curtis. A young man was just being wheeled away, and another brought in. Dr. Curtis nodded at her, his eyes ringed with fatigue lines, and he took the report from the nurse.

Lee looked down at the patient and drew her breath in hard. He looked a lot like Tom—the same black hair and square jaw, the same heavy-lidded eyes that were closed upon pain. She held onto the table to support herself against a wave of terrible depression. It wasn't Tom, it wasn't, she told herself, and looked for all the little differences in his features, and found them with only mild relief. The similarity was enough to cause her pain.

But Dr. Curtis was giving orders now and she drew herself to attention. Anesthesia was applied at once, and the doctor pulled back the blanket on a bare, mutilated chest. Lee glanced away, nauseous, and caught the eye of the nurse who frowned her own horror in return. The doctor covered the chest with the blanket and raised the man's eyelid's one by one. He lifted the limp and tender wrist of his patient and listened for a pulse.

Lee watched him drop the wrist and draw the blanket up over the pale face. The anesthesia was unnecessary. The man was already dead.

The doctor rang for the outside nurse who came in promptly and wheeled away the body. All four people in the operating room looked at each other over their masks, their eyes reflecting unspeakable pain . . .

During the next few hours, there were two other casualties and several successful operations. Lee was so involved in the work that she had no time to think of her fatigue or of her shock at the first death she had seen in the operating room. Dr. Curtis gave quick orders which registered as an action in her mind, and they all performed with the precision of dancers. It was after midnight when they completed the night's work.

Dr. Curtis thanked Lee for her help and said he would get somebody else for the following night, if it was necessary. Glad for that, she went up to her room with slow footsteps. It began to come over her again, a great depression; the face of Tom was renewed in her mind, but now attached to the face of death. She knew she would cry in the darkness; she would have to hide her tears from Maggie.

But Maggie wasn't there, and Lee went to the open window to feel the cool night air on her face. Looking out, she thought with bitterness about the people who were killing all these young men.

"I hate them," she whispered.

The sound of her own voice made her aware of her loneliness, her distance from home. For a moment she wished she had never come to Saigon. She wanted Tom; that was her only reason for being in this brutal place, she thought. And that one reason was bearing no fruit.

She had no more information about his whereabouts than she did when she was in Oregon. Again the face of Tom returned, mixed with the face of the young man on the operating table, and Lee began to cry.

She lay face down on her bed, sobbing bitterly, when there was a knock on the door. Lee sat up quickly, brushing the tears from her face, and asked who was there.

"Khai."

Lee's first reaction was one of anger and rejection of the girl whose husband was a Viet Cong. She almost told her to go away, when her feelings shifted again to one of acceptance.

"Come in," she called in a hoarse voice.

Khai entered timidly and paused when she saw that Lee had been crying. Her face expressed immediate concern.

"Shall I go away, Lee?" she asked.

"No—please—sit down."

Lee watched Khai go and sit on the edge of Maggie's bed, and the familiar ways of her friend drove away some of the bitterness that remained. She blew her nose and managed an encouraging smile. But Khai did not smile back; instead she looked carefully at Lee.

"What has happened to make you so unhappy?" she asked. "I see you are feeling some hostile things about me . . . is it true?"

"No—yes—for a minute I did," Lee admitted, her face blotched from her tears, "but it's all gone. I'm just tired, really."

"You were working tonight. Did something go wrong?"

"I guess it did," Lee said, feeling the tears again; but she swallowed them, and said, "It was a patient who died. He looked like Tom."

"I'm sorry," said Khai. "I think I understand your emotions."

Lee looked at Khai's face that concealed so much fear and pain, and she was sure that Khai did understand, after all.

"Well, let's forget it," she said.

"It's better like that," Khai agreed and smiled at Lee.

"Now I feel very silly coming to you with my worries."

"No, please don't. Tell me."

"It's just that I hope you won't speak of Pham and his affiliations. It would be difficult if I were associated with them—and, of course, I could be." She lowered her gaze and said, "I don't expect you to tell anyway. I just became alarmed tonight, thinking about it. That's all."

"I won't tell. Maggie will do her best to find out, but you can be sure I'll keep it a secret," Lee said emphatically.

"Poor Maggie. She's so frightened of losing Bennie, and I believe he loves her but finds her very difficult."

"I'm sure he does," Lee said.

"Well—it's late—and we're both tired and nervous," Khai said, standing up. "This is what happens to women without men."

"You've got a point there," Lee laughed.

When Khai left, Lee was glad that she had stopped by. She didn't want to feel hatred toward anybody when her energy could be put to constructive use. She went to bed and slept without dreams.

CHAPTER 6

The next day there was very little for Lee to do in the operating room. The men from the night before who had been severely wounded were being sent in a jet back to Denver or to the hospitals nearest their home towns. A kind of quiet settled over the hospital as the medical staff took a breather between emergencies.

When Lee went into the hall, she was stopped by a marine named Dick and a Catholic missionary, Sister Agnes; they asked her to accompany them to the Vietnamese hospital nearby. Lee agreed, glad to have the opportunity of seeing in the flesh those patients she lectured about on the *Charity*.

The sun was already high and hot in the sky, and the three of them got into a jeep with a canvas awning on top. They drove away from the hospital and Saigon with warm, dusty wind blowing on their faces. On the way Dick explained what the marines were doing to help the Vietnamese win the war.

"We just move on into a village," he said in a Southern drawl, "and teach them methods of self-defense and self-improvement . . . They need a real strong feeling of security before they'll fight ol' Charlie. That takes time. At first they're real suspicious, but then we show them how to clean up the sanitary conditions and irrigate the paddies after the monsoons are long gone, and ladies like Sister Agnes here teach the young children and the li'l orphans how to read 'n write."

Lee was impressed by his desire to help the people

help themselves and by the calm dedication of Sister Agnes. She looked out at the countryside and saw some signs of bombing in the red soil that was blasted apart in the middle of green fields. Tall bamboo trees waved in a slight wind. Through the trees she got her first glimpse of the plain hospital that housed many Vietnamese victims of the war. She knew that Khai made regular visits to this hospital and she wondered how the medical staff at this hospital would feel about her visiting them.

It turned out that everyone was very friendly. While Dick and Sister Agnes went their separate ways, Lee was given a tour of the wards in the rudimentary hospital. Two Vietnamese nurses showed her around, and since they could speak very little English and Lee could speak little of their language, Lee learned about the hospital mostly from sight. She was very shocked by the children's ward, where war orphans played or sat in bed, their faces reflecting the fears they felt. Many of them were sickly, their skulls or limbs covered with open sores. She almost cried at the sight of a little girl whose smile peeped out of swathes of bandages; and the sight of the older people was less horrifying afterward.

When she met the Sister and Dick in the jeep again, she found they had brought a little Vietnamese boy along with them. His name was Hiem and he looked about eight years old. Lee sat in the back seat with him, and tried to make conversation, but his face was solemn and showed how lost he felt.

"Where is he going?" she asked Sister Agnes.

"We'll take him to the station hospital and see if he can find his mother there. If he can't, I'll take him to the orphanage. He needs some care. Scurvy. But it isn't severe . . . He's in shock, I believe."

Lee's heart went out to the little black-haired boy beside her. He sat in a rigid, nervous way and jumped when she took his hand. But she held on tight as they drove back along the dusty road and slowly he relaxed against her, his eyes blinking against fatigue.

When they arrived at the hospital, Hiem didn't want to let go of Lee's hand, but the Sister pried him away and took him inside. She vowed to see him again, as soon as possible, and went on out to the *Charity* for her afternoon's work. Her emotions were raw for the rest of the day, as her thoughts kept returning to Hiem and his loneliness. For the first time she felt the life behind the faces on her slide screen, as she pointed with a rod at the symptoms of tropical diseases. Her classes went quickly and in an ordinary way, but Lee felt different, a little closer to the heart of the war.

She was very grateful when Johnny called and said he would be right over. Luckily Maggie was eating dinner when Lee got ready to go out. She wanted to avoid her roommate as much as possible, and she slipped into a lavender colored dress as fast as she could.

Johnny was in his uniform still and he looked especially strong and attractive. He took Lee's arm and led her out into a waiting taxi.

"Well," he said when they were settled. "How are things with you?"

"Changing all the time," Lee said. "But how about you? It must have been a terrible week."

"It wasn't very pretty," he admitted. "But at least I'm still in one piece—for whatever it's worth."

"It's worth a lot," Lee said.

"If you think so, I'll agree."

They smiled at each other in the semidarkness of the cab, and Johnny began to describe some of the action on the border. He told her briefly about night bombings and crawling across open fields, about dropping from parachutes and fighting hand-to-hand. However, he told it in a way that showed he wanted to forget it. His voice was almost toneless and constrained. Lee could see that he had suffered, but she would never know how much. She only knew that she was very glad to be with him again, and she tried to believe that it was mostly because of his connection with Tom.

They went to a hotel restaurant in the American district of Saigon. It was filled with officers and civilians, and a small stage was set up in the back of the room for music. When they came in, only a juke box was playing.

Lee heard some familiar songs from home—Sinatra and Streisand—which made her very nostalgic.

They both ordered gin and tonic and leaned back to relax and forget the war for awhile. Johnny told Lee about his childhood on the streets of New York and his first girl friend at the age of five, and he asked about her.

"My first boy friend was Tom—I was thirteen when I first saw him—not a very lucky age, I guess," she said, "but that was it."

"Lee," Johnny said, leaning forward on his elbows to speak more closely to her, "I think he must be dead. I did some asking around. That was the general consensus."

"People have been wrong before," she said, lowering her gaze from his. "But thank you anyway."

"I've never met a girl like you. Most of us just take what we can get and leave it at that . . . but you want more, don't you?" Johnny asked, his voice inquiring and gentle.

Lee nodded, knowing that he wasn't making light of her feelings.

He said, "Well, I don't want to change you, and I don't want to be the one who puts the knife to your dreams. Please don't ask me to do that."

"I won't," she said. "We won't talk about it any more."

He leaned back again and Lee watched as a pretty girl with blond hair, wearing a grey suit, stopped beside their table to talk to Johnny.

"Great to see you back," she said. "I hear you were your usual wild and daring self."

"It's all accident or showing-off," Johnny remarked in a sarcastic way.

"Can I have an interview sometime?" she asked and glanced quickly at Lee.

"I'll be around for a few days. I'll call you," he said.

The girl squeezed his hand and slipped away.

"She's a correspondent," Johnny said. "Quite a brave little gal at that. She'll go out in the bush if she can find a good story."

"She looks so fragile," Lee said. "I never would have guessed."

"Underneath she's got a heart of steel. Not like you, Lee," he said.

Lee didn't comment, for she felt put off by the girl correspondent without knowing why. Their dinner arrived and Lee tried to fill the emptiness inside her with the delicious roast beef, but it didn't work. At a nearby table a nurse that lived on the same floor as she did was holding hands across the table with a handsome LCDR. The nurse looked radiant and just the opposite from her usual efficient self at the hospital. Whenever Lee glanced at Johnny, she found him watching her with a small smile playing about his lips, as if he knew exactly what she felt.

"What are you thinking?" she asked him at last.

"I'm not thinking. I'm wishing," he said.

Lee blushed and looked towards the stage where a young army officer was settling down at the piano, another at the drums, and a third came on with a trombone. The voices grew lower in the restaurant as a young woman in a blue sequin dress went up to the stage and took up the microphone. There was a clatter of applause and the musicians began the first few bars of the national anthem. People put aside their food and drinks in order to rise, and Lee found herself standing close beside Johnny as they all sang. For Lee and everyone in the room the song was filled with a meaning that it never had at football games or the like at home. Its original meaning in the line of battle came soaring from the throats of those present.

Suddenly there was a terrible crash that shook the tables and floors and split a wall wide apart. People screamed and fell close together. Wood and cement flew in every direction, knocking people down, and the lights went out.

In the blackness and screaming Lee felt herself being grabbed and pulled to the floor. Johnny covered her head with his arms and told her to stay calm. All she knew was that she felt no pain, that she was safe. The clamor around her was deafening and strange, a combination of the worst she could imagine. But Johnny held her

61

hands against her face and whispered soothing words to her, telling her to wait until it was all over and everything would be all right. She heard voices crying and finally in the distance the wail of sirens that meant relief rather than sorrow.

"We should do something," she said, and tried to move away from Johnny.

"No, no, stay down . . . it might happen again," he said, holding her fast.

"But they're hurt—those people!"

"Stay where you are, Lee. Help is coming."

She relaxed as best she could, but the sound of voices in pain was almost too much to bear. It seemed an eternity before flashlights beamed into the room and footsteps, assured and efficient, circled the room. Johnny released her and they stood up, only to see in the dim lights that the room had been blasted on one side, that several people had been felled by flying stone and wood. More sirens emerged in the distance and with them there came more men with stretchers and beams of light. Lee did what she could, as did Johnny, who was experienced as a medic in the field of disaster.

Together they lifted away laths and blocks of cement, revealing the wounded underneath and calling over the men with the stretchers for help. Others as fortunate as themselves went to work as well, and nobody needed to speak in order to know what to do. The wounded were taken to the station hospital at once, while those who were dazed were taken into the street and consoled as best as possible.

Lee herself had to calm the girl correspondent, who was shaking all over and weeping. They stood on the cool street as stretchers passed by and a crowd gathered around.

"Terrorist bombing," was on everyone's lips.

"I want to go home!" the blond girl wept on Lee's shoulders. "I want to go home!"

"It's all right," Lee said. "You're all right. You can go home any time you want . . ."

And she looked at the curious faces around her in the

flashing beams of light for some sign of Johnny. She knew he wouldn't go away without her, but still she found she needed to know where he was in order to feel completely safe. The girl blew her nose and began to pull herself together as the last ambulance drew away from the curb nearby. She looked around over her handkerchief for a familiar face, as did Lee, and then she caught sight of one and ran off, leaving Lee alone.

The crowd was full of chatter around her, words that she couldn't understand, and the hotel windows were ablaze. Only the ground floor had been damaged and remained in blackness. Lee shivered and clasped herself, when she felt an arm around her waist. She turned quickly and saw Johnny next to her.

"Let's go, kid," he said.

She followed him through the crowds and down the streets which grew increasingly quiet the farther they walked. He kept his arm around her waist as he looked for a pedicab, and Lee leaned against him, feeling shaky now that it was all over.

"We seem to run into trouble whenever we go out," he said. "I wonder why."

"We certainly don't ask for it!" Lee laughed.

"No, that's true, although neither one of us would be here if we didn't like some kind of adventure."

He waved to a cab and they ran over and climbed inside. Once settled in peace again, Johnny sat back and looked at Lee from a distance.

"You okay, kid?" he asked.

"Yes . . . you?"

"When's your day off?"

"Well, tomorrow," Lee realized with surprise.

"Okay. How will we make up for this? Think of something nice to do."

"Why, we could go visit Charles Marcel," she said. "He asked me."

"Alone?"

"No," she smiled. "He's married, and asked me to bring a friend."

"Okay. He's the one with the rubber plantation, right?"

63

"Khai's half-brother."

"That sounds fine to me. Let's plan on it . . . I'll get a car."

They discussed when and where to meet all the way back to the hospital, and Johnny asked the driver to wait while he walked Lee to the door. There he took her hands in his and smiled at her.

"Sure you're all right?" he asked.

"I'm sure." She looked down at their hands and felt a short wave of dizziness and uncertainty. "Why do you keep seeing me, Johnny?" she asked.

"I could ask you the same question," he said. "Couldn't I?"

"I guess so," she said in a soft voice.

"Okay. So go on to bed."

He released her hands and opened the door for her. Lee slipped inside, again bewildered by her feelings of fear and confusion when she left him.

* * *

Lee was sorry to find Maggie waiting up for her. Dressed in fluffy slippers and a pink nightgown, she was sitting on her bed doing her nails. She barely looked at Lee when she entered the room but cleared her throat.

"Well," she said. "Out with Johnny again?"

"We went—"

"I heard about the bombing," said Maggie. "I went downstairs to check and see if you were okay. They said you were. Must have been a bad scene, though. Hm?"

"It was awful. How are the people?" Lee asked, removing her shoes.

"Some are pretty cut up. No casualties yet." She glanced at Lee quickly, "Your dress got ripped in back. I can sew it up."

Lee looked at her dress and saw that the seam was ripped and the hem was stained. She removed it and let Maggie examine it, although she only wanted to be in bed, asleep.

"I'll do it tomorrow," said Maggie. "How's Johnny?"

"He's fine."

"I guess you're still kind of mad at me . . . about Khai, I mean." Maggie looked at Lee with suspicion. "How did it go? Did you find out the truth?"

"Yes. So now we can forget it."

"How do I know?" Maggie muttered.

Lee left the room for the bathroom, where she washed quickly and promised herself not to get bugged by Maggie's pressures. The last thing she wanted, after the terrorist bombing, was cross-examination by her roommate. She still felt weak from the shocking event and she knew herself well enough to fear that she would lose her temper if she were questioned too much.

"Did Johnny find out anything about Tom?" Maggie asked when Lee returned.

"No. Nothing new."

"You're a funny one. You act like you don't give a damn if the enemy is right under your own nose. They say the nicer a Vietnamese is to an American, the more you can be sure he's with the Viet Cong. And Khai is a very sweet girl."

Lee slipped into her nightdress, without replying, and climbed into bed.

"Nobody ever listens to their conscience talking. Especially beautiful people. But you should listen to me, Lee," said Maggie, climbing into her own bed. "You're awfully naive, you know."

Both girls switched out their lights at the same time and the only light in the room came from the moon through the window. Lee stared at the ceiling, and her limbs were tense as Maggie spoke.

"I wonder about you and this big search for Tom. It just isn't normal. You should face the facts—about Khai and Tom even. You know, it's just possible that he went over to the other side. Even if he was with special forces, he could've changed colors midstream . . . It's happened before, you know. Usually brainwashed."

Lee clenched her fists under the sheets and almost screamed at Maggie, she was so angry and shocked at what was being suggested. But she controlled herself and said nothing. She waited for more, listening to the distant chirp of the cicada outdoors and Maggie's steady breathing. A long silence fell in the dark room.

"Why don't you react?" Maggie asked at last.

Lee said nothing but stared straight ahead.

"I know you're not asleep . . . Lee, I've been in the service fifteen years. I haven't gotten a ribbon yet. If you had been hurt tonight, you would've gotten a ribbon and a Purple Heart. It's all luck. Everything is luck." Her voice caught on a small sob and Maggie went on with tears in her words. "You've got the luck of beauty. I don't. I can't stand myself . . . and I can't stand being near to you and Khai. You're both blessed with beauty and there's not a man alive who doesn't want you for it. Not one man. Bennie's no exception."

"Don't talk that way, Maggie," Lee said into the darkness. "You shouldn't compare yourself to others like that. If Bennie didn't like you the way you are, he wouldn't see you all the time . . . Just try to relax about it. You're the one who thinks about it like that, and you alone."

"Don't be so romantic," Maggie snapped. "I know the score. I don't blame Bennie either."

"Well, I don't blame him for getting impatient with you for thinking about yourself as if you were some kind of freak. Why don't you give him some credit for choosing to see the girl he likes? That is—you. Just give him some credit for taste."

Maggie sniffed away her tears and didn't reply to Lee's remarks. Lee waited for her to protest and repeat how she felt about herself, but Maggie said nothing. They lay in silence for awhile and went to sleep at last.

CHAPTER 7

At ten o'clock the next morning, Johnny arrived with an army jeep to pick up Lee. They both wore light clothes for the country, and the canvas roof of the car kept away the hot sun. Lee was excited by the prospect of a full day away from work, especially with Johnny.

They drove northeast and had occasional glimpses of the Mekong River and junks with mustard-colored sails that floated along the brown water. The rice paddies they saw were bright green under the sun, and one or two water buffaloes could be seen above the tops of green reeds, along with the cone-shaped hats of workers.

"That river travels 2800 miles," Johnny said. "All the way down from the Tibetan highlands. It reminds me of the Mississippi, it's so wide and muddy-looking."

"It looks very peaceful."

"You'd never know a war was going on, would you?" He smiled at her from behind his dark glasses. "Appearances are deceptive, as they say. I hope you realize that."

"Are you deceptive?" she asked lightly.

"A little, I guess. Would you ever guess that I've killed a lot of people?"

"No," she admitted.

"I guess women don't split themselves into lots of different people the way men do. I'm shocked that I killed so many people, but I'll do it again in a week or so."

"Tom used to say that about himself too," Lee said.

"It's a pretty common remark around here."

Lee looked at Johnny and realized how little she knew him. Now that they were away from the city and the hospital, it struck her that they were really strangers to each other. If it weren't for the war, they would never have met each other. She remembered how protective he had been the night before when the bomb shattered their temporary peace of mind; in a crisis people became friends very quickly. This was a new experience for her, since she had led a sheltered life, and she was afraid of it. She only knew him as a part of the war; and, now that they were leaving Saigon for a social occasion, Lee was tongue-tied.

She looked at the emerald green rice paddies that they passed and realized that they would be near Khai's home town. The landscape was so foreign to Lee that she began to see that even her Vietnamese friend was only a friend by chance. The two girls came from different worlds . . . but how different did that make them?

"We're a lot alike," Lee heard herself say aloud.

"Us?" Johnny asked with a smile.

Lee laughed, "No! I was thinking of Khai."

"Her husband is one of the smartest the VC have working for them."

"You know that?"

"Sure. Most people do. That's not surprising. Most of the families here are split by the politics. Nobody expects anything else."

"I wonder what Charles Marcel's connections are," Lee said. "He could be any number of things."

"Well, we're almost at his house now, so we can begin looking for clues."

The trip was much faster than Lee had expected. She saw the landscape change from the rice paddies to a grove of rubber trees and then a regular forest of rubber trees. Johnny slowed the car and turned up a driveway that was narrow and dusty. Flowers labored under the hot sun. The road wound uphill for quite a way. The farther they drove, the more exotic the plants became, and it was only by the sight of an old Peugeot parked at the end of a tiny path that they knew they had arrived. They had been driving for more than an hour, Lee realized with surprise, and her bones were cramped when she stepped into the sun.

"They must have had a Vietnamese architect," Johnny said, taking Lee's arm. "We'll have to walk a little way to find the house."

Birds were singing in the trees and flowers that bordered the narrow path, and between the gray flagstones large bugs were rushing around. The air was very still otherwise. The path was winding, but finally they walked around a wind screen onto an empty terrace. More brilliant flowers bordered the terrace and beyond them was a low stone wall. Johnny led Lee through a small opening in the wall, as if he had been there before, and she found that they entered a pavilion circled by bamboo trees. Lee heard voices farther on, and they walked in the direction of a rock garden beside the low white house. There they saw Mimi Marcel, dressed in a light dress and a bandana, pulling weeds out from between rocks, and her husband in a deck chair nearby. He looked startled at the sight of Lee and Johnny, but his expression quickly turned to pleasure.

"Mimi," he said, "Here is a friend of Khai's—Lee Knight—"

And both of the Marcels came forward to shake hands. Lee introduced them to Johnny and saw that they were sincerely pleased to have visitors.

"Let me show you the house, and then we can have some lunch," Mimi said to Lee. She was an attractive dark-haired woman in her forties, and her accent was very slight, she spoke such good English.

Lee followed her from room to room in the one-story house. It had many picture windows looking out onto rock gardens and beyond them the plantation of rubber trees. The house was designed for coolness, it seemed, and the rooms were immaculate and sweet with the smell of flowers. They went into the kitchen where Mimi collected glasses, ice, and bottles for drinks, and she kept remarking on her pleasure at having them as guests.

"I'm glad that Khai has found a friend at last," she

said. "She's always been very independent, you know, not like Khoung."

"I don't know Khoung at all," Lee said, curious to hear more.

"She is very affectionate and gay. She's like my own child. It is Khai's influence that makes her study medicine, you know. She really wanted to go back to Paris with us. But Khai has persuaded her that the war is her responsibility, and so she studies."

Mimi shrugged a little sadly and led Lee through the living room onto the terrace where the men were waiting. They were protected from the sun by an awning, but even so it was very hot outside. Lee sat beside Johnny, who was very relaxed and satisfied.

"As you enter by the path," Charles was saying, "you are supposed to experience different aspects of nature which are like the state of your soul . . . That is what they say."

"I've seen this design before," Johnny said, "but mostly among Buddhists."

"Yes, well, that makes sense."

Mimi fixed each of them a drink and sat down on the ground at her husband's feet; he rested his hand on her shoulder. Their natural affection and hospitality convinced Lee that they weren't involved in any plot for overthrowing the government. She felt herself relax in their presence and found Johnny smiling at her as if he understood.

"As the saying goes, many Buddhists are my good friends," Charles said with a smile, "Being a Catholic puts me in a special minority here, but only in the eyes of outsiders. I try to avoid prejudice of any kind."

"That should be hard," Johnny said, "especially when you've lived here for so long."

"It is hard, but so are most convictions." His face darkened and he looked out at his garden with sudden gloom. "Both Saigon and the Viet Cong are fighting for my property. They send agents to bargain with me every week. Now the Americans must defoliate the land and that takes care of that. There isn't any choice left, and,

70

when that happens, all you have left is a conviction. My conviction happens to be fairly selfish—survival—and so I'll go elsewhere, back to France . . . My father was a political animal, but I am not."

"Charles is an artist," Mimi said. "We'll show you his studio before lunch."

"My work is sold in Paris, so it won't be so bad going back," he said, and stretched his legs before him with a quick smile. "I might as well retire to the city in my old age."

"Is there a lot of VC activity around here?" Johnny inquired.

"Of course. For all I know it might be very wise to defoliate my rubber trees. I don't pay much attention to them these days anyway."

"Well, let's talk about something else," Mimi suggested. "I think Lee should see our favorite pagoda some day."

"I'd love to," Lee said.

"Well, we'll arrange it."

They went to see Charles's studio, which lay in a grove of palm trees far beyond the house. It consisted of one large, sun-filled room, and some of his recent paintings were hanging on the walls. They were very colorful and showed an oriental influence that was not surprising to either Johnny or Lee. It seemed that Charles's whole life was devoted to the culture of the Far East, and during lunch it became more and more obvious that he was not involved in politics.

"Khai suspects me of all sorts of things," he said, "but that's because of her pride. She knows that her family is in danger right now, poor girl, and she wants to find blame not connected to Pham. She loves him a great deal, and he loves her too. With all the marines in her mother's back yard, she is right to suspect some violence."

"Pham is far away, isn't he?" Lee asked.

"No. Khoung says he's around. She has heard. But she doesn't know where he is."

"Poor Khai," Lee sighed.

They had a delicious lunch of cold chicken and salad

and plenty of white wine that made all of them drowsy. Afterward they all went to separate rooms to nap, and Lee dozed lightly on her back. The birds singing outside the window made her dreams carry her into a world that was half memory and half new. She saw herself with Tom in her mother's garden at home, with birds singing all around, and he was looking at her with the dark, gentle gaze she loved so well. But as they looked at each other, she began to see his eyes glaze and his face stiffen into a distant smile, and he fell into her arms. She woke up in tears, unnerved by the strange surroundings.

"It's not true," she whispered. "He's still alive."

But still she was full of dread. The dream might as well have been real, for even awake she saw the way his face changed from the living to the dead and felt him in her arms as if he were there still. She brushed the tears away and got up to leave the room when she heard a knock on the door.

"It's Johnny."

She opened the door and he looked at her as if he could see traces of her dreams.

"Are you all right?" he asked. "We ought to be starting back."

"I'm fine."

They said goodbye to the Marcels on the terrace and promised to return soon for a visit to the pagoda in Khai's home town. Lee couldn't shake off the effects of her dream but felt sad at saying goodbye to the older couple, as if they were her parents, again on the wharf in San Diego. She liked them and felt sorry for them under the circumstances of moving away for good. She could see that Johnny liked them too, and she wished she hadn't ruined a perfect day by having such a terrible dream.

"Why so sad?" Johnny asked, when they were driving back to the main road.

"Too many thoughts," Lee said.

"About Tom?"

She nodded her head and looked at the passing trees for help. She didn't want to break into tears now.

72

"I'm out in the bush again tomorrow," he said, "This has been a very good day. Maybe we should just go out with the sun, and that way we'll keep out of trouble."

They reached the road, and as they turned toward home Lee looked at Johnny with concern. She was frightened by the thought of him going away again to fight, in case he would never return. His strong, tired face and his brown hands resting on the wheel were beginning to be familiar to her, but more than that she was ready to depend on him as a source of understanding and sympathy. She liked his quiet ways and admired his ease in every situation. She couldn't compare him to Tom, who was a gregarious and often nervous person. She only knew that her feelings for Johnny were very strong in their own way.

"What will you do when you leave here?" she asked him.

"Go back to medical school," he said. "I'm getting kind of curious about such things. It's good. I don't want to jump into a swamp anymore."

"Did you ever want to?"

"For awhile I was tempted. When I floated down under that big white tent, I'd see all sorts of easy ways out down below." He grinned at her quickly. "I guess I never saw any real reason to keep on going."

"Do you now?" she asked.

"Sure. Medicine, girls, wine."

"Are you in love with a girl at home?" Lee asked.

"Nope, and I never was," he said, "but I guess I could give it a whirl one of these days."

"You should," she said. "It's not so bad."

She smiled at him and their eyes held for a little too long. Lee looked away quickly, her heart pounding. For that brief second, they had seen into each other's hearts, and now she knew it wouldn't be so easy between them again. They had seen too much for a simple friendship.

As the warm wind whipped against her cheeks, Lee looked out at the rice paddies under the flat blue sky and she thought of Tom again as she had seen him in her dream. She had to know the truth, she realized, and she thought of one last way she might find out; it was a fact she didn't really want to have, but now something gave her the courage to pursue it.

"Is it Johnny?" she wondered. It was a question she couldn't answer, and when they said goodbye to each other outside the hospital, she promised herself that she would know the truth by the next time she saw him.

"Take care," she said to him.

"You too."

He kissed her forehead and walked away. She went into the hospital with a feeling of dread and loneliness.

* * *

Lee went directly up to Khai after work the next day.

"Will you have lunch with me?" she asked, "I'd like to talk to you."

Khai nodded and looked at Lee with curious eyes. "Is something wrong?" she inquired. "You look a little worn down today."

"Bad dreams," Lee said, managing a smile.

They walked together into the cafeteria and collected their trays and food. The sun was streaming into the room through the eucalyptus trees outside, and the girls decided to eat outdoors. They went out onto the green lawn where the sun warmed their faces and hair.

"Now what is on your mind?" Khai asked, squinting at Lee through the bright sun.

"Johnny and I went to lunch with the Marcels yesterday."

"And so? They are usually pleasant hosts," Khai said.

"Yes, it was all very nice. But I came back in a terrible mood . . . I've got to find out the truth about Tom, Khai," Lee said, tugging at the grass around her. "This uncertainty is bad for everyone concerned."

"You mean Johnny and you?"

"No!" Lee protested at once. "I mean me and Tom's family and—oh, I don't know—"

"And you want me to help you find out the truth?"

"Could you try?"

74

"It would be easy to try," Khai said with her eyes on Lee, "but it was a long time ago. They may not remember him—or know him now."

"But they might."

"If he was a special case, yes, they might," Khai said, and she reached out to squeeze Lee's hand. "I'll do my best."

"Thank you," Lee murmured.

Ever since she said goodbye to Johnny, Lee had been feeling unusually depressed. Now her mood picked up a bit, with Khai's calm nature helping her. She had reached a point where she would, at last, believe what she was told about Tom's whereabouts; she couldn't go on dreaming much longer. She still had hopes that he was a prisoner of war in North Vietnam, that she would see him again soon. At the same time she could now believe in his mortality and accept the fact of his death.

"Isn't casualty a terrible word?" Lee said to Khai. "As if it were a casual matter!"

"It's like the word mission that they use nowadays. It used to mean an act of charity; now it means the opposite."

"Oh Khai, you must be suffering much more than I," Lee sighed.

"Not yet. But I dread the future, it is true."

"What do you think will happen?" Lee asked.

"I am afraid that Pham is involved in some activities on the Vaicon, near my home," she said. "They are already asking the people to evacuate, including my family. Khoung says they are already putting up barbed wire around the hamlet. If Pham is in that area, it makes me very sad."

"Don't you ever know where he is?" Lee asked.

"I get messages. That's all. Just love words." She smiled and looked down at the grass. "That isn't much use."

"No."

"We better go in."

"This is my last day on the *Charity*. They're starting to cruise the coast tomorrow," Lee said, gathering up her tray. "And then I'll have a ward of my own here."

"Oh good," Khai said quickly. "I want you to meet a new little friend of mine. Hiem. He is an orphan."

"Hiem!" Lee cried. "Why, I was planning to look him up."

And she explained to Khai how she had met the little boy at the hospital. Khai was ecstatic about him, and her eyes lit up as she told Lee stories about him. Lee was glad to see that Khai had found an object for her affections at last, for she knew that her friend was lonely without her husband.

"I'll do what I can about Tom," Khai said, when they were separating. "But tomorrow you must visit Hiem. He will be good for you."

Lee promised that she would and hurried out to meet the car that took her to the ship. The day was clear and sunny, and, feeling happier, Lee looked out the window at the busy streets of Saigon with some of her old interest. She thought of the bombing in the hotel, as they passed it by, and it made her think of Johnny, far away in the field now. For a moment she imagined herself arriving on the *Charity* at some distant port, where Johnny would be waiting. But then she shook away the thought and went over her lecture for the day, her professional self again.

CHAPTER 8

Lee worked very hard for several days. With the change in her schedule, there came more contact with people, and at night she studied in the hospital library. Her new ward was for post-operative care, so that she was dealing with the same wounded men she saw on the operating table in the morning. The treatment was fairly new to her, mostly consisting of applying pain-killing drugs and changing casts. She found that the men were courageous even under conditions as boring as lying in a hospital bed.

The problem of tropical malaria among foreigners was being discussed by almost everyone at the hospital. Fear of an epidemic was extreme and many new precautions had to be taken. All these new things required study from Lee, and she enjoyed her quiet evenings in a corner of the library after facing so many worries all day. Some doctors were being flown over from home to deal with complex diseases, and Lee met some of them each night at dinner. Each one came in for a couple of weeks, leaving behind an expensive office and many patients, and the experience affected them strongly.

One of them said to Lee, "It will be hard going back to New York after this. We're very prosperous over there, you know, and very lucky."

And another said, "I was given a patient with tuberculosis; he was in terrible shape. His wife brought me the nest of a sea swallow, made with the bird's saliva, and the man took it and relaxed . . . I never would have found such a cure in Santa Barbara."

Lee found out from one of them that many of the

people in small villages ate such things as cows' heads, birds' eyes, bats' wings, dog entrails and dried cockroaches. No wonder, she thought, that smallpox and leprosy are still thriving here! But more and more she wanted to visit a village, and she looked forward to Johnny's return when they would go with the Marcels to see one.

Her main pleasure came from visiting Khai and Hiem. The little boy was learning English now with Khai's help and his scurvy had been treated easily—with good, vitamin-packed meals—so that he was healthy again. Since the Sister's orphanage was overcrowded, he was being kept around the hospital until he could be placed somewhere else. Day by day he became a source of pleasure to the wounded men, who played with him and tried to teach him new slang words.

"Cool," he would say, when he liked something, or "No kidding."

His eyes held a fear of loss, but he was quickly affectionate and ready to laugh. His attachment to Khai was very strong, and many people thought he was her son.

One day Lee was having lunch on the lawn with Khai and Hiem, and the two girls were watching him run around at a distance; he was learning how to somersault with the help of a G.I. with a broken arm.

"You seem much happier since he came here," Lee said.

"I am. But what will I do when he goes?"

"I don't know," Lee sighed, and laughed. "Maybe you shouldn't let him go!"

"I've been thinking that," Khai said. "I'd like to adopt him."

"Could you manage it?"

"I don't see why not," Khai said. "It would be good for both of us."

"Then do."

They watched in silence as Hiem turned head over heels on the grass and got a playful spanking from the soldier. Khai laughed, and Lee realized how important it was that Hiem stay. With all the disasters in the air, the child was like hope itself. Lee didn't ask Khai about

Tom. It was an unspoken understanding that she wait for Khai to give the final word, and the silence made them even closer friends.

That night in the library Lee thought about the past few weeks since her arrival in Saigon. Many things, good and bad, had happened; but one of the best surprises was her friendship with Khai. It seemed like a fragile thing, however, though Lee wasn't sure why. It must be the difference in our backgrounds that makes me feel like that, she thought. But that wasn't quite right. What held them together was the same situation that would split them apart: the war and the men they loved. She couldn't completely separate Khai from her husband and she was sure that Khai couldn't separate her from Tom and his affiliations. That was the terrible truth. When it came right down to the heart of the matter, each girl would side with the man she loved and thereby renounce their own friendship.

It saddened Lee to think of that. She was very fond of Khai and knew there was a real understanding between them. But that night she wrote a letter to her best friend at home, describing the hospital and the city as if she were a tourist. It made her feel strangely guilty to write that way, as if she had betrayed her loyalties to Khai. But she shook off the feeling and got ready for bed.

Maggie came in with a crash of the door, her cheeks flushed and her eyes bright.

"Hi!" she said in a cheerful voice.

"Hi . . . What happened?"

"Nothing. Why?" She went to the mirror and made a face at herself, "Ugh. I was having so much fun, I forgot all about my make-up."

"You look very good as you are," Lee said, observing Maggie more closely. "In fact, you look great."

"Oh come off it, Lee. That's what Bennie said too. You both must be laughing up your sleeves . . . Look. No rouge and hardly any mascara."

She pointed at her own face. But her complexion was naturally glowing and her eyes, very blue, were very bright. It was the first time Lee had noticed the natural qualities that were pretty in Maggie and she was very curious as to what had caused the happiness to bring her beauty out.

"What happened?" she asked again.

"We went all around town in a pedicab and my hair got all mussed, and then we went dining and dancing and it was just lots of fun," she said and kicked off her shoes.

"Well, take a look at yourself, Maggie. You look lovely and radiant," Lee said, "and you should know it."

Maggie went to the mirror again and scrutinized her image.

"I don't get it. Bennie said it too. Maybe your little lecture the other night did some good . . . I decided to give him some credit, you know, and sort of stopped thinking about myself so much. This is the result. I forget my make-up!"

"Well, forget it again. You look wonderful," Lee said and climbed in between the sheets.

"I might as well," Maggie said, her face serious. "He goes away again in two days. Tomorrow's our last night —for awhile, God willing."

"Poor Maggie. You'll be sad."

"I guess I really love the guy, fat as he is," she said with a quick laugh. "And by the way, he wanted you to come along out with us tomorrow night. Just for dinner or something."

"I'd like to," Lee said.

"I kind of told him what you told me, and he thought it was just fine."

"You asked for it," Lee said with a smile.

While Maggie undressed, Lee tried to sleep; but her mind was filled with thoughts and memories. She dreaded the day when Khai would come to her with the word on Tom, and at the same time she longed to hear the words that he was fine. She wondered how other people could accept things so easily, when she seemed to fight against accepting them. She remembered Tom's parents and how they received the news that he was lost in action. Brokenhearted, they believed what they heard, as did everyone else. But no body was ever returned, and to Lee that meant hope. She never saw the signs that he was dead, so why should she believe that he was? At home her family and friends considered her search futile and even silly. They expected her to give up her job in Saigon and return home at any time, sadder but wiser.

"If he is dead, what will I do?" she wondered; and she had to admit that her first reaction would be to pack up her bags and go back home.

Then she worried about Johnny, as she did frequently these days. He came into her imagination when she was least expecting it, and then she would see his face and hands very vividly and sometimes hear things he said. It upset her that she should be under the spell of his personality just the way everyone else was. But she had to admit that she was, and she remembered the look they gave each other by chance and felt weak and afraid. Most of all, she wanted him back safe.

* * *

She was glad to be going out the next night. Her mind was burdened with medical questions, and she realized that the best way to shake them off would be to get away from the hospital environment. The memory of the terrorist bombing stayed with her as she dressed that evening in a full skirt and white ruffled blouse, for the dress she had worn still hung in the closet with a rip in its hem. The whole experience had the quality of a nightmare not connected to anything else, and, although there had been no casualties, she knew she was lucky to be around.

Maggie followed her advice and wore a simple sheath dress and very little make-up. This style softened her and brought out her natural points of beauty, as well as making her less self-conscious. Together they went down to the lobby to meet Bennie, who had a pedicab waiting for them outside. The night was especially warm and the sky was milky with stars. Maggie's mood was quiet, for she dreaded Bennie leaving the next day.

"What's on your mind, Mag?" Bennie asked; and Lee noticed that he seemed nervous himself.

"You know what's on my mind," Maggie said with a sniff.

"Lee, you'll have to keep our spirits up," Bennie said and began to bite his nails.

Lee wondered why they had brought her along and decided she would leave right after dinner. She felt sorry for them both, but felt there was something unusual in Bennie's behavior; he was usually easy-going. The fresh night air was reviving her and the creaking pedicab rocked her into a pleasant sense of freedom. Already the streets of Saigon were familiar to her, but they never ceased to enchant and fascinate her. As they came into Me-Linh Square, the big white buildings reminded her of the colonial atmosphere of Washington, D.C., and the round fountain reminded her of pictures of Paris. She thought of Charles Marcel as part of the culture here, although he had absorbed the Vietnamese culture himself. His own paintings might fit into the National Museum here, they were so heavily influenced by the Vietnamese. She looked at that building—a round pagoda in a heap of white flowers—and promised herself a visit inside one day. The art works of this country must be beautiful, she thought, and could understand Khai's feelings of national pride.

They drew up before the officers' club in the Brink Hotel, and Lee decided she'd better cheer up her companions.

"You should go dancing after dinner," she suggested.

"It won't make any difference," Maggie said.

"Come on. I reserved us a table." Bennie urged them inside ahead of him and they went to a table in a far corner. "There now. I'll be right back."

"Where's he going?" Maggie asked.

"I don't know. Poor guy. He's upset, isn't he?"

"He's acting like a bunny," Maggie remarked.

Lee smiled at her and noticed that theirs was the only table with a bunch of flowers in the center—white orchids with purple stamens—and she pointed this fact out to Maggie.

"Maybe they do it with reserved tables," she said.

They could see Bennie talking with the waiter, his stocky figure gesticulating towards the kitchen and then toward their table.

"Maybe he's lost his mind," Maggie said.

"Oh well. Enjoy it while you can."

Bennie came back to the table then and dropped down heavily into his chair. His face was flushed and his laugh uneasy.

"What's up, Honey?" Maggie asked him with concern. "You okay?"

"Sure, just fine . . . Here's the waiter. Let's get some drinks."

They all ordered gin and tonic, and Lee leaned back to watch the others in the room. A juke box was playing songs from home, and many men were in uniform. Lee thought of war movies she had seen and tried to draw Bennie out of himself by mentioning some scenes from *From Here to Eternity*.

"Don't remind me," he said. "It makes me homesick."

"Homesick!" Maggie cried. "And you don't even have a home to be sick about."

"Hey there, pal," Bennie called to a man nearby, and he jumped to his feet and left the table.

"I don't get it," Maggie muttered, "but it makes me jumpy."

"I never saw him this way before," Lee said.

"Neither have I."

The two girls sat in silence, waiting for Bennie to return, and when he did they all ordered dinner. He insisted on the best—"for old time's sake"—and ordered a bottle of wine as well. Maggie could barely eat, she was so upset by his behavior, and Lee could see she was near to tears. Bennie kept looking at her with round eyes as if she were a complete stranger, and then he would squirm around in his chair with a sigh.

Poor Maggie, Lee thought, remembering how happy and hopeful she had been the night before. Now it seemed that Bennie was reacting against her, and Lee could see her becoming increasingly downcast and self-hating. She wished she could do something to change the course of the evening, but her presence was strange enough as it was.

"Why did they ask me anyway?" she wondered.

The waiter came and took away their plates, and at that point all the blood rushed out of Bennie's face. Lee thought he was going to be sick. He was fumbling around in his pockets, and Maggie was so hurt by then that she was pretending nobody existed outside herself.

"Are you all right?" Lee asked Bennie.

"No! Yes, I mean," he said in a rush and forced a smile at her.

"Maybe a dessert would sweeten you up," Maggie said under her breath.

"Dessert's coming," Bennie retorted.

"I don't want any," she snapped.

Lee looked away, embarrassed by their nervousness. She saw their waiter coming out of the kitchen with a white cake and aiming for their table. She looked at Bennie, and saw that his face, drained of color, was bent toward something in his hand. Then he kicked Maggie under the table.

"Hey," she cried, bewildered and cross.

"Here," he said.

He handed her a small box, just as the cake landed on the table, its white icing crossed with pink letters that said: MAGGIE BE MINE. Maggie's hands were trembling, her eyes glistening, as she opened the box; she didn't even see the cake. Lee watched, her heart in her throat, as Maggie drew a big diamond ring out of the box.

Bennie mopped his brow with a handkerchief and stared dully at the cake before him. Maggie burst into tears, which drew attention from the people in the room, and Lee saw Bennie reach out and take her hand, shoving the ring on her finger with shaking hands. Maggie just sobbed: "No, no, no," into her fist and shook her head, while a few people gathered around the table with smiles. Bennie got slapped on the back, and Lee saw with relief that the color came back into his cheeks and he began to chuckle.

"Congratulations!"

"You did it at last!"

"You old fool."

Everybody crowded around, while Maggie began to pull herself together and took the handkerchief that Lee held out to her. But then she saw the cake and burst into tears again, which brought cheers and laughter from the crowd. Bennie had sunk back in his chair, relieved and smiling, and Lee found herself laughing with everyone else.

"I don't believe it," Maggie said at last, blowing her nose.

"Well?" Bennie inquired. "Will you or won't you?"

Everybody cheered as Maggie jumped up and gave him a big hug, squeezing his head against her bosom, and soon she was cutting the cake into several little slivers for everyone to have. Lee smiled as she watched and found herself really liking Maggie for the first time in ages. She kept showing the ring around and staring at it, wide-eyed, and bursting into happy laughter. It was her night, and it reminded Lee of the night that was hers two years before when Tom came to her home at Christmas with a ring. She looked down at it, shining on her finger, and her vision clouded.

"I should go soon," she said to herself.

The other people retired to their own tables and Maggie snuggled up beside Bennie while they ate their cake. They looked very much in love and very relaxed together now. When she had finished her cake, Lee told them she had to go, and Bennie took her outside to find a cab.

"I'm very happy for you," she told him.

"Well, I'm sure glad you came along. You mean a lot to Maggie, you know, and it helped me having you there too . . . I thought I was going to pass out, I was so scared," he said with a laugh.

"Be careful, Bennie," Lee said. "And come back soon."

She climbed into a pedicab by herself and headed back

for the hospital, her feelings raw and uneasy. The dangers were all too real; any one of these men might die. She wondered what the meaning of it all could be and why there weren't more civilized ways of arriving at the same conclusions. From what she had learned about this war, the cultural and political complexities were outstanding. The Vietnamese were as brave as the Americans, no matter which side they were fighting on, but their idea of victory was national unity and under the circumstances that was an almost hopeless goal.

She hated to see the wounded men, that was all, she decided since she understood so little of political games. And she prayed that Bennie would be all right, so Maggie could fulfill her dreams. She looked up into the stars as they neared the hospital and saw five planes flying in formation under the twinkling blackness. She tried to imagine the men inside them—who were they? where did they come from? what did they want?—but they disappeared before her imagination could answer the questions.

She hurried inside, tired from the wine and her work all day, and took the elevator to the third floor; she was eager for rest. But when she opened the door of her room, she saw Khai waiting there. Lee snapped awake at once, while supporting herself against the door. She guessed why Khai was there.

CHAPTER 9

"Have you been waiting long?" Lee asked.

"No. Maybe half an hour," Khai said. "I browsed through this book."

She held up a medical textbook and then put it down again beside her on the bed. Lee entered the room fully and removed her shoes; she sat down opposite Khai on Maggie's bed. Her mouth felt dry and her heart was pounding.

"Well," said Khai, lowering her gaze. "The news is bad, Lee. I have his dog tag, as you say, and full proof that he was captured and that he died."

She stood up and handed Lee the silver tag that bore Tom's identity. Lee held it in her closed fist, speechless. It pressed against her engagement ring and dug into the flesh of her hand.

"He landed across the border in his parachute and was engaged in hand-to-hand combat alone. He was badly wounded, but they took him back for questioning. They had no time to inflict any tortures upon him or get any information from him. He died in Cambodia then." Khai recited these facts in a low voice that was almost toneless. "They keep a record and the tags of those who are brought in for questioning, you see."

"I see," Lee whispered. "Thank you—for finding out."

She waited for Khai to go, but instead she saw Khai sit down again on her bed, her hands folded in her lap and her head bent. Lee felt numb and didn't even feel the pain from her pressing the tag into her hand, where it drew blood. She held her breath, as if she were sinking underwater, against the pain that began to grow in her. She remembered a time when Tom kissed her there on the palm of her hand and she stared at the same place dumbly.

She looked at Khai and said, "You'd better go."

"No. I'll see you to bed."

"I'm not tired."

"Yes, you are," Khai said and she stood up and folded back the sheets on Lee's bed.

"I'm not tired," Lee repeated in a harsh voice.

She looked at Khai with sudden hatred, as the one who had brought the final word, as the one connected to the enemy. She watched her sit down again, slim in her blue *ao dai*, and had a desire to hurt her, to scream at her. *It's your fault*, she cried inside, and clenched her fists in fury against her friend. Never had she felt such hatred and despair. She directed it all at Khai, who sat with her face down, in silence. She stared at her with anger and pain, and finally in a rush of rage, she threw the dog tag at Khai. It hit the far wall and slipped down behind the bed. Lee burst into tears.

"It's your fault," she sobbed. "Go away, go away!"

But Khai stayed where she was, motionless, speechless. Lee put her face in her hands and sobbed more and more helplessly, and she cried Tom's name many times in vain. Finally Khai came over to her and put her arm around Lee and spoke soft words in her own language. At first Lee resisted, feeling pangs of hatred for Khai, but then the hatred was replaced by waves of emptiness before the fact of Tom's death. The emptiness was like the sand on a desert absorbing all the rain and sun away. She felt small and hopeless in the face of such a barren world, for she now accepted the fact that he was gone forever. Lost to her all this time she had kept him alive in her mind, she would never see Tom again.

As the waves of sorrow and emptiness continued to grow in her, she felt less and less resistance to Khai. Weak, she wanted to be put to bed by a gentle soul, and Khai's voice was soothing in her ears.

"Let's get you ready for sleep," said Khai, "and I

brought some pills along with me . . . I won't go until you're asleep, Lee."

Lee nodded her head dumbly and stood up to remove her clothes. As she dropped them off, Khai put them away and handed her her nightdress. Lee climbed between her cool sheets at last, her mind dizzy and lost in darkness. Khai shook out a pill from a small jar she had carried with her and gave it to Lee with a glass of water. Then she turned off the light and sat on the edge of the bed beside Lee.

"I don't hate you, Khai, I hate the war," Lee whispered.

"So do I."

Lee closed her eyes and her face became tortured with grief again. The tears poured down her face and she thought about the next minute, hour, and day as almost impossible to confront. Deep down she had been ready for this moment, had even suspected the truth, and that is why she reacted so totally now. But she wanted to leave Saigon at once and go home.

Through her tears in the darkness she could see Khai sitting in a position that revealed her depth of understanding; hands clasped in her lap and her head bent, she knew there was nothing she could say or do. But for Lee her presence was a comfort. She began to feel the effects of the pill in her bones, and she let the tears pour freely down her cheeks.

When sleep came at last, it was deep and dreamless. But she woke in tears to the sunlight and saw that Khai was gone and Maggie lay asleep in her bed. Lee wondered how fast the night had passed and how she could have slept so well, when her grief was so great. Luckily at least, it was her day off, and she could seek a quiet place to be alone.

"I want to go home," she thought again, wishing for her childhood bed and the consolation of her parents' love.

She lay still for awhile, until the tears subsided, and then she got up and dressed to go out. Through the windows she saw that it was a hot day, but she tied on a bandana and wore cool clothes so that she could be protected from the heat. She put on dark glasses that covered her swollen eyes and went down the elevator to the lobby. She stepped out into the sun.

"I want to go home," she thought again.

She began to walk down the drive away from the hospital, and she heard the cicadas chirping in the dry grass all around her. Long shadows shivered at her feet until she reached the main road to Saigon. Then the trees receded, as she walked toward the city. Green fields bordered the road, and at the far end of them stood tall mahogany trees. They were very still and strong in the quiet air. Lee looked around her, seeing the countryside for the first time so closely, feeling the alien soil near by. The sun seemed to drain away her energy for grief and dry her emotions away. But the quiet of the landscape beyond the scuff of her feet on the pavement made her aware of herself as a foreigner.

"What am I doing here?" she wondered. "Now that the search is ended, why am I here?"

The sky blazed over her head. She watched a car approach and then disappear. She remembered a road in Oregon like this. Wild roses blew in the bushes at the end of August there and she used to walk along it on her way to school. In the summer crickets chirped like the cicadas now. She could take a plane via the Philippines and be there tomorrow. That was a comforting thought. This was the landscape that held the body of Tom. Monsoons and summer-hot sunlight would have covered him deep in the earth for many months. She thought of him parachuting down, down to his destruction, and all his youth and ambitions disappearing as if they had never before existed.

"They all were right," she thought bitterly, "when they accepted the words on the paper."

She could see, way ahead of her, the rooftops of the city beginning. Today they struck her as sinister and full of secrets. Riots were increasing by the day, riots among religious and political factions that sought peace by war. In comparison with calm suburban towns in

America, Saigon seemed to her like a monster, prepared to strike at any moment.

She walked for another half hour, at a slow pace, attempting to come to terms with the time that lay ahead of her. Without love, life was hardly worth having. The dream that nourished her for years was laid to rest with Tom, and she looked into the future without a trace of joy. Many extreme reactions came to her. She would live like a nun and devote herself to her work until her death; or else she would go wild and abandon her profession for pure fun. But as she entered the city, bustling with people as ever, her reaction seemed almost foolish.

She smelled the hot *ñuoc man*—rice and fish—and the oriental cakes and sweets being sold around her by snack merchants. She stared at the soda-pop rainbows of wagon venders. She heard the voices of venders all around her. She walked more quickly, without looking into the faces around her, and headed for the port of Saigon, without thinking why. Crossing wide boulevards and sidewalks, she followed the route of her first journey to the hospital.

When she got there, the sun was at its peak of heat, and the cool breeze from the water was a relief. Lee sat down on a bench facing the harbor, where sampans and tugs were anchored around the docks. She watched the sea birds flying around in search of fish, their long beaks biting into the dark water. This was where she had arrived, and today she thought of leaving. Her head felt clear and her sorrow was a part of her feeling of independence. She thought of returning to a regular civilian hospital in Portland where she would be far from the atrocities of war.

She stared out at the boats, and her eye caught sight of an American flag flying on the bow of a small navy boat. At first it reminded her of home and made her long to be there, but then a strange feeling took hold of her. She watched the flag fluttering in the breeze and it made her think of all the wounded men she had been treating for so long now. They still needed care. They would continue to need care for an unknown period of time. That was why she was there: to care for them.

Lee realized that with surprise, for her original purpose had been so strictly personal. She had a duty outside herself now and it filled her with a new sense of freedom. She wouldn't go home. She would stay in Saigon, where all her training and experience would be most useful. Out of the ashes of her dream, she would construct a full life for herself, for there really was no choice.

"If none of our plans come off, make it with somebody else, my darling, and that way the dream will last." Those words that Tom had written to her returned, and with them a feeling of hope mixed with sadness. She had no choice but to rise up as a better person. To do otherwise would be to lose all faith in a world and a duty beyond herself.

Lee stood up from the bench and walked away from the port of Saigon, lonely and grieving, but revived by new hopes.

* * *

It was hard to keep the hopes alive in the days that followed. More and more wounded men came into the operating room and ward, and Lee's attention was fully focussed on them during the day. At night, in her exhaustion, she had time to brood on her personal loss. Memories of Tom plagued her: the way he walked, laughed, talked, the way he touched her the first and last times they were together, and the way he enjoyed planning their future. She wrote letters home, revealing the facts and her own decision to stay in Saigon. At night she watched the flag being lowered outside the hospital and it revived her sense of purpose. But always she returned to the grief and solitude induced by Khai's news. She wore her diamond ring on her right hand now, and whenever a group of men were brought to the hospital, she prayed she wouldn't find Bennie or Johnny among them.

Her lunch hours were still spent with Khai and Hiem

out on the hospital lawn. Those hours were inspiring to Lee. Like Khai she learned from the small boy that life had its simple and happy side as well as its disappointments. He was beginning to lose his moments of fearfulness and to adapt wholly to the new situation. He and Khai were together in the world, it was decided without any legal form, and he began to call her Mother naturally. He had plenty of men around him to replace his lost father too.

"Khoung will join us for lunch today," Khai told Lee in the Nurse's Station one morning. "I am afraid she has bad news."

"You should see her alone," Lee said.

"Should I? Perhaps. She left the *Charity* on the Vaicon to work at the dispensary at home. That's why her visit worries me. Perhaps you are right. Why don't you join us after a half hour? . . . I want you to meet her, in any case."

Lee agreed to do that, but she was afraid for Khai now. It was all too possible that her hamlet could be involved in a Viet Cong raid. The Americans had set up a barbed wire perimeter around the hamlet, as well as around the dispensary. The people were evacuating their homes to some extent, although many of them stayed where they were, having nowhere else to go. Either the Viet Cong planned to overtake the hamlet, or else the Americans planned to strip the area of all enemies. Or both. It could be a head-on collision, resulting in disaster for the hamlet.

There were only two patients that morning in the operating room, both of them requiring standard treatment. Lee watched Khai over her mask and saw that her eyes were ringed with lines of fatigue. Lee imagined Khai lying awake worrying all night and realized that she had been pretty selfish these past days. Khai's situation was horrible: her husband against her family in a life and death conflict. What could be worse?

"And there's nothing she can do to change the course of events," Lee realized. "Absolutely nothing."

Lee ate her lunch inside that day and talked with one

of the temporary doctors from home, an elderly man named Stone.

"I think you women are admirable," he said to Lee. "It's a nerve-wracking job in a nerve-wracking city. In the last war the nurses weren't so far away from the familiar. Europe is part of the American culture. But this is different . . . You must be very brave."

"No," Lee laughed, "I'm not at all."

"You won't go out into the bush, will you?"

"I don't think so," she said.

But she wasn't sure. The idea of working in a village dispensary appealed to her, since the work would be varied and close to the people. There was some talk of sending nurses out into the countryside now, and Lee listened with interest. She was determined to complete her eighteen months of commissioned duty and she wanted to make it as interesting as possible. But it was also frightening to imagine being so close to the war itself, and she had no craving for medals or promotions the way many girls did.

After lunch she went outdoors and saw Khai and her sister sitting under a eucalyptus tree with their trays and Hiem playing close by. Approaching them, Lee could see that Khai's fears had probably been realized. Her face showed strain, and Khoung was talking to her in a nervous way. Lee stopped beside them, uncertain whether to join them or not.

"Lee—hello," Khai said.

"Hello," her sister smiled up at Lee.

Hiem came running over to pull her skirt; he wanted to show her a model boat he was building in the sun. She smiled at the girls and followed him to where the model was lying—a replica of an AKA—and she stayed with him for some minutes, admiring his craft. But finally she heard Khai call her name and she returned to the shade of the tree.

"Khoung says you are an excellent teacher," Khai said, trying to be polite even though her face showed how distracted she was.

"I stayed on board the boat," said Khoung, "until I got

home and then I stayed there to work. I know many things now. Thank you."

"It must be more absorbing there than on the boat," Lee said, kneeling on the lawn.

"It is very useful," Khoung said, and glanced at her wristwatch. "But I must go now."

"All right," Khai murmured.

Khoung asked her sister in Vietnamese what she was feeling.

"*Com Thu*," said Khai.

Lee understood; it meant hatred. She looked down at the grass as the sisters said goodbye to each other in their own language and promised to be in touch with each other soon again. When Khoung was gone, Khai sighed very deeply, and Lee saw her rub her eyes unhappily.

"What happened?" she asked.

"All that I expected," Khai said with a quaver in her voice. "My mother will not evacuate . . . and other things."

"What other things? Pham?"

"Never mind, Lee."

"But you're suffering. I'd like to help you."

"You can't."

Khai looked at Lee with an expression that she recognized. It was her own look of hostility toward one connected to the enemy. As an American, in Khai's mind she was the cause of much trouble and would be the cause of more.

"I'm no more involved than you are, Khai," she said in a low voice.

"You wear a uniform. Today I see it. Yesterday I didn't."

"It's true," Lee said with sadness.

"I must go," Khai said and gathered the trays together. "I have to work."

Lee knew that it was her afternoon for working at the Vietnamese hospital she had visited. She didn't protest, but stood up beside Khai; they both watched Hiem from a distance. He was the real victim of the war in that he was innocent. Time hadn't connected him to cruelty so far.

"Hiem!" Khai called.

He stood up and stared at them with curiosity. Then he gathered up his materials and followed them across the lawn. Lee looked back at him with a feeling of sadness, and then at Khai the same way. Would they ever cross these boundaries for good?

"I wish you would talk to me, Khai," she said. "Your friendship has been so important."

"So has yours. But it is too difficult. We see in each other too many conflicting duties."

"I can't believe it."

"You are innocent. Americans are innocent. You are a nation of children. Don't you see? Things are not good and bad, but contain many elements, and your soldiers have adopted the methods of the French, who raped us and left us . . . How can I be your friend?"

"You have been until now. That's how."

"You don't understand."

"Why doesn't your mother go stay with the Marcels?" Lee asked.

"I begged her not to," Khai said, with a glance at Lee.

"You're very stubborn, Khai."

"You don't understand."

"Well, I can feel for you even if I can't understand you, and I will wait until you feel better . . . Then we'll be friends again."

"Will we? Perhaps."

They nodded goodbye to each other at the door of the hospital, and Lee watched Khai and Hiem walk down the long avenue of trees side by side. They both looked very small and vulnerable from afar and she tried to believe that Khai's feelings against her wouldn't last. But she knew that Khai was stubborn, and that she didn't understand many of the reasons for it. It hurt her to admit that, but she knew it was true. She was a foreigner in a ravaged country, and she was bound to her own people because of her ignorance. She wished that Johnny were there, for she wanted to talk to him.

CHAPTER 10

Fortunately Johnny returned, free of wounds. Lee received a call from him the evening of his arrival, and they arranged to meet later on. She returned to her room with a feeling of pleasure she had lost for a long time. Maggie was reading on her bed, a pair of diamond-studded glasses pushed down on her nose. She looked very studious but threw aside her book when Lee entered.

"Is he okay?" she inquired.

"Yes. Thank God."

"I hope you'll be happy, Doll," Maggie said. "You've been nervous lately. I guess it isn't surprising, under the circumstances, but it's always important to remember the good times when the bad times are on you. I just lie on my back and dream of Bennie and the times we were real happy together."

"Poor Maggie. You're the one who should be nervous," Lee said, going to her closet to choose a dress for the evening.

"It's funny—but now I can understand what you were feeling like. I think if anything happened to Ben, I'd go right out into the bush looking for him. I just couldn't stand not knowing."

"Don't even think of that, Maggie," Lee said with a frown. "It's too awful to imagine . . . As you say, remember the good times."

"As if I could forget," Maggie said with a sigh from deep inside.

"The worst of it is that you have to go forward. You can't stop, and you can't go back. It's a one-way street," said Lee.

"I know, but which way is forward?"

"You tell me," Lee laughed.

She selected her lavender dress that Johnny and Tom had liked, and laid it out on the bed while she made herself up. She realized that she and Maggie were talking about a real dilemma. How to give up the past for the sake of an unknown future—that was the hardest thing she had experienced. If Maggie had to go through the same thing she had been through, she really pitied her. And she wondered if she was really through it after all. Still haunted by the news about Tom, she had thrown all her energies into her work. But tonight she would be confronted by a new personal experience, and her knees felt weak.

"I wish I didn't have so many feelings," she said. "They get in the way of everything I do."

"We're all like that—trapped," said Maggie. "My Dad used to say 'You got to learn to live with yourself, since you're stuck with yourself until the very end.' It's a pretty scarey thought."

"But true, I'm afraid."

"I never thought one person could make such a difference," Maggie murmured with a glance at her engagement ring. "But he can. Right?"

Lee nodded and slipped into her dress. She wondered if she and Johnny would meet another violent scene on the streets of Saigon. The situation was getting worse daily, so almost nobody felt safe in town. It was strange being hated by people for reasons of nationality, Lee realized, because it was something she had never known before. The hatred had nothing to do with personal feelings or actions; it was irrational and fierce. It made a person suspicious, often without reason, and she could see that suspicion growing in the people around her. Maggie's attitude towards Khai was no longer unusual in Lee's eyes, and Khai's attitude toward herself was no longer unusual either.

She and Maggie had dinner together that night, and then Lee went into the lobby to wait for Johnny. Sitting there, she recalled the night she met Charles Marcel;

and now she hoped to arrange another meeting soon. Day by day her curiosity grew about the Vietnamese people and how they lived outside of Saigon. She planned to ask Johnny to take her on a short trip to visit one of the hamlets—if he wanted to see her again. Her heart was pounding faster than it should, as she waited for him to arrive, and she scolded herself for taking everything so seriously.

He was dressed in casual civilian clothes and his face was very dark from the sun, so that his smile was very bright when he greeted her.

"Hi, kid," he said and kissed her on both cheeks. "You look beautiful."

"So do you," she said with a quick laugh.

She followed him out to a jeep he had commandeered, and he helped her in with a squeeze of her hand.

"Well now, what's new?" he asked, revving the engine.

"A lot of things," she said.

"Tell me every one of them."

"I want to hear about you first."

He headed the car down the dark avenue of trees onto the main road into Saigon, while Lee squeezed her damp hands together nervously. The wind whipped refreshingly against her cheeks, but still she felt warm with a nameless anxiety.

"I honestly don't want to talk about my war experiences," Johnny said. "I'll do enough of that in my later years. My grandchildren will suffer."

"Okay. I won't ask any questions then. It's good enough that you're still in one piece."

"I'm glad about that myself," he said with a smile.

"I won't tell you anything until we're settled down—"

"But then a bomb will drop."

"I forgot . . . Well, let me take the risk."

"Okay."

They entered the dark streets of the city and drove away from the Americanized section of the city to a restaurant called Caprice's. It was a hangout for special forces, known for its pretty girls. Johnny had reserved a corner table for them, and they pushed their way through crowds of Vietnamese officers, Green Berets, and colorful girls to their quiet corner. Johnny ordered them cooling drinks at once and drew his chair closer to Lee, so they could talk more intimately.

"You seem very cheerful tonight," Lee said in a soft voice.

"It came over me after I talked to you. I was afraid you'd turn me down. It's been a long time."

"Yes, it has," she agreed and looked at him with disbelief. He was really back—safe! Deep down she had been worrying for him, and only now that he was beside her did she realize how deep the worry was.

"You've been on my mind, Lee," he said. "Did you get any news?"

"Yes," she said, and told him quickly what Khai had said. It was hard to tell him, because she knew he cared, and that made tears very easy. But she held back any signs of emotion.

Johnny didn't say anything for awhile but watched the people around them as if he hadn't heard what she said.

"I hear Bennie proposed to old Maggie," he said at last.

"Yes. She's very happy."

"You'll be happy too, one of these days," he said and smiled at her. "I'll make sure of that."

"And what about you?"

"My turn is coming up," he said with a grin. "I can wait."

They ordered dinner then and talked about their visit with the Marcels and plans for a trip to see the pagoda. Johnny explained to Lee that much of the trouble in the country was between the religion that represented political alliances too. Buddhists were naturally more inclined toward the Far Eastern cultures, and Catholics were inclined toward Europe; this made the church and the state much more involved with each other than they were at home.

"Being a half-caste, like Khai, leads to terrible trouble," he said. "She's torn between two entirely different worlds.

It will be especially hard for her to find any kind of happiness."

"She's completely rejected the French side, though," Lee said.

"I doubt it."

"Well, you're probably right too."

They finished their dinner quickly and decided to go for a walk. Johnny said he was tired after the past days of constant warfare, and so they planned to make it an early evening. Outdoors the streets were quiet and for Lee they were as mysterious and enchanting as ever. The tropical trees and fine architecture made a weird contrast to one another, and she found herself feeling more liberated than she had in a long time. Worries about work, patients, and herself were set free, like birds from a cage, and her mind felt easy. Johnny held her around the waist, as they walked, and she leaned against him without fear.

"Is it the liquor?" she wondered. She felt like singing or running.

"Stop a minute," Johnny said, under a street lamp, and he turned Lee around to face him. "I like you with your hair down best."

He reached up and began to draw the pins from the security of her dark hair. One by one the strands came loose, falling to her shoulders and shading her pale features. She watched his smile of sarcasm turn to one of pleasure, and she had to smile back.

"It's so nice," he said.

He ran his hands along her arms until she felt weak inside and her shyness began to melt away to desire. When he drew her against him, she didn't resist, but felt that it was right and good to be so close to him. She held him as he held her until their lips met and they kissed with passion. All her fears and sorrows fell away from her in his arms, and she felt him caressing her hair as if his touch were some magic gesture that would soothe all pain.

"Lee," he whispered in her hair, "I love you."

"Me too," she sighed and then laughed. "Not me—you!"

They laughed against each other and began to walk a

few more paces before stopping to kiss again, and again. They held tight to each other all the way back to the hospital in a cab, and when he took her to the door they met again, with passion, as if they were afraid it would be the last time. Lee couldn't speak and neither could he. They kissed goodnight and parted reluctantly. When she went inside, Lee felt weak, happy, and lonely all at the same time; she wanted to beg forgiveness from Tom but somehow she felt sure he wouldn't have wanted it any other way for her.

"Dear God, let him live," she prayed before sleep, and now her only fear was of the war in the hills of Viet Nam.

* * *

For the next two days, Lee was absorbed by her work in a completely new way. Her happiness overflowed into all that she did, and even the men in her ward remarked on her attitude.

"Lee's got something going," one said.

"I never saw a woman smile that way who wasn't smiling that way for somebody special," another said.

"Come on, Lee, who's the lucky guy?"

Her joy was infectious and a new admission, a boy of nineteen with the blond hair and expression of an angel, arrived with his guitar. He would strum and sing, and all the patients would join in, while Lee watched on. She was glad to see them reviving in spirit, and many of them knew songs from the backwoods of America that made them all homesick but happier for remembering.

Each night she saw Johnny, and their attachment to one another grew stronger and stronger. He took her home early enough to be ready for work in the morning, and on the third day, she was grateful for that because of a difficult operation: open heart surgery on a young man. The whole morning was devoted to this patient and Dr. Curtis worked with painstaking care on this rare case. Khai and Lee held their breath, as they listened to the thump-thump of the heartbeat in the room.

For Lee it was especially fearful since her feeling of responsibility for the wounded was growing daily. Now that she loved one of the men, she knew in every part of her that each man who was hurt was also loved by someone far away. Somebody cares, she repeated to herself over and over again, somebody cares. The lonely courage of the men was amazing to her, for the rewards were small in comparison with the deeds they performed. Nobody at home would ever know what these men had suffered, and even she was ignorant of the war itself.

She tried to restore her friendship with Khai, but the girl was aloof and quiet. The day of the open heart surgery, however, brought a feeling of closeness to all of those involved. It was a success. Dr. Curtis kissed the three nurses, one by one, and congratulated them on their calm efficiency.

"By now you must be ready to do it on your own," he said.

"Oh no!" they all protested.

Lee smiled at Khai and asked her to join her for lunch. Khai nodded and they went to the cafeteria together.

"Outside? Where's Hiem?" Lee asked.

"No, let's eat inside today. He's with the Sisters."

"Why?"

"They're deciding, officially, whether I should have him or not," said Khai with a trace of bitterness.

"Well, of course you should!"

"I know. I am sure I will too. It's just very silly, all these official routines, you know."

They sat down at a table by a window and Lee looked out at the sunny lawn with thoughts of Johnny.

"Charles called me last night," Khai said, "He found you were out. He wants you to go with him to my village tomorrow."

"Luckily, I can," Lee said with pleasure.

"He remembered it was your day off tomorrow . . . you made a very good impression on him and Mimi. So did Johnny. Is it true that you and he are seeing one another?"

"Yes," Lee said with a smile.

"That's good. He is very nice, I think."

"He is . . . How about you, Khai? Is everything the same, or better?"

"Worse," she said and tried to smile. "You forgot it could get worse. I am afraid of what will happen to my mother any one of these days."

"You should make her evacuate," Lee said.

"I will not have her going to the Marcels for protection."

"Isn't that her choice?"

"She never had any principles."

"But this is hardly a time for principles," Lee cried.

"It is always a time for them," said Khai in a cool voice.

"You're very unreasonable, really . . . Was she in love with your father?"

"I don't know what you mean. She gave in to him. That's all . . . She says she loved him, and she stayed with him until he died. But she was just being a coward."

"Are you sure?"

"Yes."

Khai looked unhappy as she spoke, although her voice showed conviction. Lee looked at her, wondering where she developed these feelings of anger, but then she remembered what Johnny had said about being a half-caste. Khai had obviously chosen somewhere along the line to take sides and to stick with one side right to the end. Lee realized then that many Americans she knew had done the same thing. They had broken off their identity with another country in order to be absorbed into the whole American culture, and she realized it had caused pain for many of them.

"I'm very naive," she said to Khai. "You're right there. But I still believe that personal feelings are stronger than racial ones. You're making a mistake. Your mother should be allowed to go where she wants, especially when it's a matter of life and death. I don't understand how you can bear to hold onto this position of yours."

"It isn't easy," Khai admitted in a soft voice. "Not at all."

"Well then?"

"Don't push me, Lee!" Khai cried. "I don't want to discuss it."

"All right. I'm sorry."

They separated that day with more understanding of one another, but less friendship. It made Lee feel very sad. That night she talked to Johnny about it for a long time.

They were walking along the river, listening to the quiet flow of water nearby and the cicadas in the grass. The city glistened with lights along side of them, and they sat on the dry grass to look at it from a distance.

"Maybe we should talk to Charles about it," Johnny suggested. "It may be that Khai wants her mother to go, but she can't do it herself."

"That's a very good idea," Lee said.

"We can give it a try tomorrow anyway."

He put his arm around her and they sat close, watching the water and the city in silence.

"It's so good here with you, I don't ever want to go back into the bush," he said after awhile. "I'd like to stay this way forever . . . but I can't. The more I see you, though, the more a regular life attracts me."

"How do you mean, regular?"

"You know. Just you and me . . . a couple of kids. No more of this jumping, running, falling, and fighting . . . I think I'll go to medical school for sure," he said, "That's my latest decision."

"But maybe you'd get bored with a regular life," Lee said.

"Not with you there. Maybe you'd get bored."

"No . . . I'm sure I wouldn't."

She leaned closer to him feeling a chill of fear. At any time he would be going out into the field again. What if he were badly wounded? Or what if it was even worse than that? She didn't dare let her happiness reach the point of hopes, not so soon.

"Cold, baby?" he asked and kissed her cheek.

"No. Just afraid," she whispered. "I couldn't stand it if you got hurt."

"Sure, you could," he said. "I couldn't."

She tried to laugh but she felt stiff with the reality of her concern.

"How much longer will you be here?"

"I can kick the habit whenever I want," he said. "I've gone beyond my term . . . Luckily. Otherwise I never would've met you."

"I wish you'd stop soon," she said.

"Only when you do. Besides, they need me."

"I have over a year left here," she said.

"Well then, so do I."

"Oh Johnny, I wish you wouldn't keep on. We could meet later."

"Come on now, kid. It's just as bad for you as it is for me, and I'm not leaving you alone here unless I have to."

"If anything happens, I'll—I don't know what—"

"Just keep on going the way you have. Don't ever make promises like that, because they're useless. You'll meet somebody else and live happily ever after. There are lots of men in the world."

"That isn't the point. I want you."

"Well, you've got me now. So relax."

She obeyed by snuggling up closer to him and letting him caress her back into relaxation. But still she felt sad and afraid for him. She thought of Tom and promised she would try to make their dreams survive with Johnny. She looked at the city of Saigon across the river and imagined all the secrets behind all the walls. Plans for revenge and destruction were seething behind the cool white facade of the city, and she and Johnny would never understand them completely. They would always be outsiders, except to each other.

CHAPTER 11

On the way to the country the next day Charles told Johnny and Lee that his rubber trees were in the process of defoliation. He seemed completely resigned to it and explained that Mimi was spending the day in Saigon; she was arranging for their departure to France.

"She is glad to be leaving, and I am glad to be getting her away at last," he said, squinting out onto the bright dusty road. "This will be my final visit to the pagoda and then I spend a few more days at home. That will finish the story."

"How sad," said Lee.

"Yes," he agreed and flashed a smile at her in the front seat beside him, "but let's not fall into despair."

While Johnny explained to Charles about Khai's mother, Lee looked out at the road and recognized it as the one that led to Marcel's plantation. She began to feel at home with the view of rice paddies and palm trees, and even the customary heat no longer annoyed her. It was so good to have Johnny nearby, she could fully appreciate the exotic quality of the landscape. She wore a cool pastel dress, while Johnny wore his jungle fatigues and green beret after some early-morning training.

"We can see if she will return with us," Charles was saying. "I think you are right. We must do it. Enough obedience to Khai."

"She'll be grateful after it's all over," Johnny said.

"Maybe, and maybe not. She hates interference, no matter what the intentions are," Charles said. "And she may never forgive any of us for saving her mother against her will. But so much for that stubbornness . . . I am glad you thought of that."

They drove a long way in silence, each of them looking out at the still countryside. They passed the entrance to Marcel's plantation and went on along the dusty road for a few more miles. A river began to appear alongside of the road, its serpentine shape brown and colorless under the noon sun. But along its banks grew exotic flowers and plump water lilies floated from green roots along the surface. The vegetation became almost tropical with the appearance of the river, and large pointed reeds were shaded by flat leaves from higher trees. Wild ducks were waddling or swimming in the river, and in the distance rocky hillocks jutted up from the fields.

At last Lee saw the mud walls of the hamlet out in a field, and inside the walls the mud and thatch roofs. As they drew closer she saw one area of the place was occupied by low white buildings with dark roofs, evidently part of American military headquarters, and a barbed wire fence glittered around the perimeter of the hamlet. The river wound away from the road and around the mud walls, bordering rice paddies dotted with banyan trees.

Their arrival was checked by a marine at the entrance to the hamlet and they drove the jeep into a flat square surrounded with mud huts. A mangy yellow dog ran barking around the car, but he was the only sign of life around. Charles turned to Johnny and Lee.

"Let's go see Khai's mother—Luy—and then we can drive on out to the pagoda and have our picnic . . . okay?" he asked.

They agreed and stepped from the car into the hot sun. The dog was joined by another, as mangy as himself, and they trailed them across the square toward the groups of huts. Now Lee could see chickens ahead, down small paths; they ran around clucking hungrily. An old Vietnamese man was sitting on the stoop of his hut, head bared to the sun, his dry features cracked and curious. But he seemed to be alone in this quiet place.

"There's her home," said Charles, pointing to an ordinary shack.

They walked to the door of it and Charles called her name. There was a shuffling from inside and then she appeared, dressed in a dark *ao-dai*. Her hair was done the same way as Khai's: pulled back in a dark bun and parted down the center. Her face, though creased with lines of age, showed signs of beauty. High cheekbones and a pretty smile could not be lost by time. She seemed pleased to see Charles, but stood protectively in front of her door.

"*Comment ça va?*" Charles inquired after her health.

She shrugged with a smile and asked him the same. They began speaking in such rapid French that Lee could hardly catch a word; but she watched Luy gesturing toward her house and the surrounding houses with an expression of despair. Charles waved toward the car and obviously was trying to convince her that she must go with him. Finally she looked off into the distance with a sad and worried expression, and he waited for her decision, his eyes concerned as well.

"*Alors,*" she said in a soft voice, "*Je vais.*"

Charles kissed her cheek quickly and looked at his watch; they made arrangements for him to return to get her before they started back. She smiled at all three of them, her face constrained, and retreated into the shadows of her hut.

"Thank God for that," Charles murmured and took hold of their arms. "Let's go see something beautiful."

They walked back to the car, and he promised Lee a trip to the dispensary before the day was over. Mimi had packed them a cold lunch in a big basket, and all of them were beginning to need it. They drove away from the hamlet again, but this time followed a narrow road beside the rice paddies up into the far hills. Lee looked at the banyan trees, whose branches grew downwards into roots, and she saw the cone-shaped hats of workers in the green paddies all around.

All at once she saw the vermilion tip of the pagoda nestled among banyan trees. It was very old and weathered, but still noble in its structure. As they drew closer, she saw it had thirteen umbrella-like discs to its tower and its shape was octagonal; small round and square apertures formed the windows of the building. Charles told them it was built around A.D. 500 and was one of the oldest pagodas still in existence. It was very ancient in design but its interior held a temple of more modern design. They parked the car on a dusty circle shaded by the knobby green trees and climbed out with their picnic basket.

"It's amazing," Johnny remarked, looking far up the circular tower.

"We only hope it won't be bombed," said Charles. "It has survived so many wars already."

They decided to eat their lunch under the trees before entering the temple. Mimi had made them a delicious lunch with rice, fish, and chili sauce mixed together, a sort of *ñuoc mom* with the delicate French touch. A bottle of cold white wine was packed in ice among cups and plates. They ate and drank with pleasure, while Charles described the background of the Buddhist pagoda in some detail.

"Buddhism is a religion of redemption, and so the high towers represent man's freedom from earth, as well as the many stages of ancestry through which he must pass in order to achieve true freedom. There is, of course, a similar aspiration in Christianity—both religions had the concept of paradise, which has since become materialistic . . . Much of the art work you will see inside was built at the close of the Northern Wei dynasty in the mid-sixth century."

As he spoke, Lee saw the brick building transformed from a sort of accident within the context of modern life into a focal point for all of history. The landscape began to take on a look of time, and she could imagine marauding armies for centuries in the very hills in which she sat. She was eager to see the art work inside, as was Johnny, so they finished their lunch quickly, lightened by the wine, and went to the door of the pagoda. Stone carvings on the door were almost invisible; they could just make out the slender lines of a winged dragon. They went inside.

Lee saw a miracle of colors. The walls of the room were painted with brilliant murals depicting Buddha in various scenes. The room itself smelled of incense from the joss sticks smouldering in jars of colored sand. A man in a saffron-colored robe appeared from a side door, his head shaven, his face round and serene. He approached them quickly, with his hand extended to Charles, and the closer he drew, the more extraordinary his face appeared. Although the wisdom of age and meditation was written in his features, his complexion showed no lines at all.

He spoke to Charles in French, while Johnny and Lee circled the room examining the murals and stopping before a large stone Buddha in a nave surrounded by burning joss sticks. They went on to look at more red and blue and gold wall paintings, and were particularly impressed by one that showed Buddha as the subduer of the five planets. He was riding over the clouds on a red cart with five figures surrounding him. The circular strokes of the brush gave the painting motion and gentleness. Later on Charles explained the symbolism of the work to them, but first he called them to the door of the pagoda. The priest had gone away.

"He advises us to leave as soon as possible," said Charles, "He says there is a VC buildup in the rice paddies. It is expected to explode today, when the river birds fly overhead . . . Already the sect here is planning to gather in prayer."

Johnny took Lee's hand and they followed Charles around the room again, while he calmly explained the meaning of the work to them. He appeared calm in the face of danger, but Lee couldn't hide her growing fear. She was relieved when they left the pagoda and returned to the car. Already the sun was on its way down and the rice paddies were darker green and completely empty of human life. Or so they seemed. The landscape took on a sinister quality as they drove back toward the mud walls of the hamlet.

As they drew near the entrance to the hamlet, Lee saw American convoys lined up in the once-empty square. A young soldier came up to the car to speak with Charles; and as he did so, Lee looked over her shoulder

111

toward the river. She saw a flock of birds rising up from the reeds.

* * *

"Better get goin' right now," said the soldier.

"I have to pick up a citizen," Charles said.

"Well—" and the soldier looked around at the activity in the convoys. "You just keep the car right here, and go get your friend. Then get the hell out of the area."

They all climbed out of the car and walked with Charles past the jeeps and tanks and officers standing around. They went toward Luy's house, but a special forces area officer stepped forward to Johnny. Lee stayed beside him as Charles proceeded to get Luy away from her home.

"Want to help out, medic?" he asked, his face creased and brown from the sun.

"You need it?" Johnny said, taking Lee's hand.

"We sure do."

"It's sort of irregular, isn't it?"

"We got an irregular Colonel—DeWolfe. He takes what he can find."

Johnny looked at Lee, questioningly.

"Do you need a nurse?" she inquired.

The man's face broke into a smile and he looked Lee up and down with overt pleasure. "Sure thing," he said, "Come on. Let's go to headquarters."

Lee felt a mixture of excitement and fear as she watched Johnny run after Charles to tell him the news. They would stay behind, while he took Luy home. She looked up and watched the birds that filled the sky like small planes and a shiver passed through her. She could still change her mind and go back to the safety of her room at the hospital. She could still change her mind. She watched Charles, Johnny, and Luy approaching hurriedly with bags of clothing, and she went forward to meet them.

"Good girl," said Charles, embracing her quickly. "I'll speak to Khai in case you're stuck here beyond tomorrow."

"Please do."

112

"God be with you," he said to her and Johnny.

She watched him go away, with Luy hurrying after him, and for a moment she wanted to run after them. But she felt Johnny's presence close by, and she knew she had to stay with him and help out in whatever way she could.

On the way to headquarters they passed a wire-mesh cage used on the captured Viet Congs; they would sit inside, broiling in the sun, until they talked. The building they approached was small, cement, with a wooden roof. Officer Kearns led them past several small rooms into one containing a table and slits for windows. They were asked to wait there, while Kearns went to find DeWolfe and get assignments for Lee and Johnny.

"Well," said Johnny when they were alone, "This is some surprise."

"Yes."

"Come here."

She went to him and let him hold her in his arms, where he told her how much he loved her and begged her to keep out of danger. She held him tight, fearing more for him than for herself. The last thing she wanted was to leave his side, but Kearns returned with the word that Johnny should join a team of special forces out in the bush, while Lee should go to the dispensary to wait. He gave Johnny directions and led Lee outdoors again toward another small cement structure, just like the last. She wanted to cry without Johnny nearby, but she controlled herself by realizing that the situation was so bad it required all the resources of her profession.

There were several rooms containing plain beds inside the dispensary, and one room was set up with rudimentary first-aid equipment.

"Sit here," said Kearns, "I'll get somebody to join you."

"Thank you," she managed to say.

She examined the equipment, which included little more than band-aids, vials of penicillin, terramycin, and morphine. This was what she had lectured about all those weeks. She was astounded to find herself actually dealing with that same situation. One bright bulb hung from the ceiling and little light entered from the small, high win-

113

dows. Lee listened to the quiet around her, knowing it couldn't possibly last for long, until she heard footsteps in the corridor. Khoung entered the room, dressed in white. She stopped in shocked surprise at the sight of Lee, and Lee was taken aback herself.

"Why, I forgot!" she exclaimed. "Of course you'd be here. How nice."

"*Tot Lam,*" said Khoung with a sincere smile of pleasure. "Very nice."

Lee immediately told her what had happened to her mother, and Khoung expressed delight near to tears.

"Khai will be glad. I promise," she said, "Thank you, thank you."

She clasped her palms together and nodded her head with a big smile that made Lee smile too. They began to go over the equipment together, and then they went out on the steps to see the sunset. It spread in pale blue colors across the sky and gave Lee a feeling of peace. The camp seemed deserted now, so the silence in the air was unearthly. Lee listened, and now she heard the buzz of planes in the distance. Khoung glanced at her with a look of fear and Lee squeezed her hand quickly. They watched six T-28 fighter planes appear on the horizon and zoom closer and closer to where they stood. Khoung was trembling all over, and Lee felt fear herself as the planes swooped low over their heads and on by toward the rice paddies. Then they heard explosions.

"Napalm," said Khoung in a shrill voice.

"We must be calm," Lee said, as much to herself as to the girl.

But as the .50-caliber machine guns rattled in the near distance, she thought of Johnny with deep fear. Would he survive this terrible night? She could imagine the white fire exploding from the bombs, supposedly hitting enemy lines; but what if it hit Johnny as well?

"Let's go inside and wait," she said to Khoung.

"Yes," the girl agreed at once.

They sat in the little room under the bright light as the sun left the sky for the night. The sky outside was filled with crossfire from automatic weapons, and the sounds shattered the silence for a long time.

"Won't it ever stop?" Lee wondered aloud.

The time was dragging and speeding at once. She felt useless and afraid, as did Khoung. But the sounds seemed to be drawing closer now, so that screams could be heard within the roar of the gunfire. Lee stood up, not knowing what to do, and Khoung ran out of the room and down the corridor. Lee followed, hearing the air grow louder and louder with gunfire. The two girls stood at the door and saw that the air was bright with exploding fire. They held onto each other as they watched, unable to move, a cement bunker nearby explode into flames, and they saw human figures emerging from the darkness and light.

They ran back inside, uncertain what to do, and stayed inside the dispensary, waiting to be killed or called upon.

Footsteps ran up the corridor in their direction. They clutched each other in terror, as the door flew open. It was a marine.

"We got two wounded," he panted breathlessly, "Get your stuff and come on out."

Each girl grabbed a first-aid box and followed the marine down the hall, relieved to have something to do, so that fear was secondary. He waved them on away from the building and past the ruined bunker. The gunfire had retreated again into the rice paddies, and the marine led them through a hole in the mud wall surrounding the hamlet. Lee stumbled over the black-clad body of a VC as she went and felt her heart leap to her throat. They hurried through the darkness toward the rice paddies, where the long grass swept against their ankles and legs. Now the black-clad bodies were all around, and Lee and Khoung moved gingerly through the deep grass. They were going away from the gunfire, but the gunfire seemed to be lessening too. The cool air revived Lee's senses and she prayed she could perform to the best of her abilities.

"Over here!" the marine yelled from ahead. "And over there!"

Khoung ran towards the second one, while Lee ran toward the first. He was lying in the long grass, curled up on his side and clutching his stomach. She knew who he was at once.

"Johnny!"

She fell on her knees beside him, while the marine ran off across the long grass. Her breath came short, her eyes burned with tears, as she leaned over him to help. His right side was dark and moist with blood, and he looked at her from his pain with only a twitch of recognition. His own medical kit was lying beside him. From hers she removed a needle and a vial of morphine. At once she gave him a shot to help the pain and fight the infection. Then she removed a roll of bandages and tape and drew back the shirt from his flesh. His side had been badly clipped by a bullet, and the wound penetrated to his rib case, where bones were shattered. She couldn't say which organs had been affected deep inside. She only knew she would have to stop the flow of blood at once.

First she smeared the wound with ointment, and then bound it up tight, while he bit his lip against the pain that seethed throughout his body. She gave him another shot and stood up to look for Khoung. She saw the girl was standing too.

"Are you all right?" Lee called.

"He was dead already!" Khoung called back with a catch in her voice.

They stood in the tall swaying grass of the rice paddy while the gunfire diminished far away.

"Go to the dispensary," Lee called, "and wait there for the wounded. I'll join you when I can."

She watched Khoung walk back toward the hamlet, her head bent and her white dress floating in the breeze. She looked like a ghost.

"Darling," Lee whispered, kneeling again.

"Yes. You're here," he said, and his eyes closed on unconsciousness.

She kissed his lips and forehead and held his hand in hers. In the distance she heard a few spare cracks of gunfire, and then the shouts of voices. She didn't want to move; she wanted to stay with him until help came.

"He has to be all right," she whispered, but she looked down on his pale face, gratefully closed on sleep, and she knew he only had a fifty-fifty chance. Time would make all the difference.

She stayed in the long grass, holding his limp, cold hand, and she watched Americans returning to the camp, one by one, at a distance. She decided to stay where she was until somebody came to get her; she couldn't leave Johnny alone in the cold grass and night.

CHAPTER 12

It was at least an hour before someone came out into the paddy to find her. Lee released Johnny's hand and stood up to watch the approaching figure, and as she did so, she saw the body of a VC only a couple of feet away from where she was. She drew her breath. He lay on his back, in the same position as Johnny, but his whole belly was torn apart.

"It could be Pham," she thought in her horror.

She watched Officer Kearns walking with his bayonet poised for use, in case any of the bodies stirred. Lee waved to him. But she didn't dare speak for fear of rousing the dead. Kearns didn't acknowledge her, his face was grim. He looked down at Johnny.

"Dead?" he whispered.

"No. But I didn't want to leave him alone. When is help coming?"

"Helicopters are on the way, ma'am," he said.

"What happened?"

"We got them before they got us. But the area is still infiltrated, and the fighting will resume. Point is, we got some wounded inside. Not bad. But we could use your help."

"But I don't want to leave him," she whispered desperately.

"Khoung says there's a casualty out here . . . where?"

Lee pointed to the spot in the long grass where Khoung had been, and Kearns looked over there without speaking. He looked down at Johnny again.

"He came out after that one—ran into a whole nest of

118

'em—amazing he's still with us. If he lives, he'll get a Silver Medal—"

"And a Purple Heart," Lee said with bitterness, and she kneeled beside Johnny again, "We shouldn't move him without a stretcher."

"We got two medics and Khoung inside. The whirlybirds will be here any moment now. I'll send 'em out with a litter for him right off—"

"I won't leave him. I'm sorry," Lee said, taking Johnny's hand, "Please get him help as soon as possible."

Kearns shrugged, "Well, I can't drag you back, I guess."

And he walked away again, leaving Lee alone in the grass with Johnny. It was just as hard to say no as to say yes, and she felt as stubborn as Khai. But she looked into Johnny's face and saw his eyes flicker open for a second; they caught sight of her beside him and closed again. His lips had a trace of a smile on them. Already his bandages were stained with blood, and she imagined the splintered ribcase doing a great deal of damage to his internal organs. But there was nothing she could do about that, except wait.

Overhead she heard a slight buzz. She looked up into the star-filled sky, praying it wouldn't be the beginning of more warfare, and over the line of trees in the distance she saw a bulky helicopter approaching the camp. A sigh of relief emerged from her throat at once and she squeezed Johnny's hand. She reached out and picked up Johnny's medical case and his green beret, and she held them in her lap. Another helicopter followed the first and then a few more. Lee watched them buzz overhead, like giant insects, and they whirred around without landing.

She stood up to watch, as one stayed near to her area and another two entered the region of the camp; another went far off in the direction of the pagoda.

"They must be getting orders," she thought and prayed that they knew about her and Johnny.

The one overhead began to drop slowly toward the earth, and then it paused and surveyed the ground and finally dropped all the way down. A man emerged at once, with another behind him; they were bearing a litter

119

constructed from bamboo wood. They ran toward Lee, who waved at them frantically.

"One dead, one wounded?" the first man called. He was a young hospital corpsman that she had seen around before; the other was Vietnamese.

"The wounded is here," Lee said.

They dropped the litter beside Johnny and kneeled to examine him. Lee watched in great fear as they hoisted him into the litter and she handed them his kit and his green beret. They carried him away from her onto the helicopter, while she stood without knowing what to do, and then the Vietnamese ran past her to pick up the body of the dead marine. He ran past her again, as her heart pounded in fear and desperation; she didn't want Johnny to go! What would happen to him in Saigon? Would he survive?

She ran toward the helicopter and its whirring propeller, and stumbled over the body of a communist in the grass.

"Johnny!" she cried, but the door to the big steel bird slammed shut.

Tears poured down her cheeks as the helicopter began to rise again, its roar nearly deafening in her ears. But as it drew higher and higher into the sky and began to turn in the direction from which it came, the night air grew quiet, and Lee found herself alone in the long rice grass. Johnny was gone.

She walked slowly back to the camp, because there was no other choice, and she passed groups of officers and convoys without seeing them. Her eyes stung with tears. Another helicopter had landed outside the dispensary, in the small dusty square, and men were limping on board. Another circled in the sky overhead, waiting its turn to bring help. Lee passed a line of wounded men in the corridor of the dispensary; some were sitting or lying on the beds in the small rooms. She hardly saw them. She was only thinking of Johnny. Was it the last time she would ever see him?

"Please let him live!" she begged.

Khoung and the two medics were working quickly and

efficiently in the dispensary. They looked at Lee with surprise when she entered.

"Where did she come from?" one inquired over the bent head of a special forces man.

"I was out in the field," Lee said. "What can I do?"

"Take your kit down the hall and start working on the last roomful of men. The others are ready to go," he said, "Last door on your right."

Dully she obeyed. She went down the hall and found five men in need of pain-killers and a temporary bandage; she performed her duty quickly. From her years of training, she had learned to make automatic expressions of cheer and solace that had nothing to do with the real way she felt. Now she saw that they had good effects, her smiles and remarks, although she herself was miserable.

"Johnny, Johnny," her heart kept repeating, "please be all right."

And finally when the group of men were prepared to take off in the helicopter, she returned to the dispensary and asked what to do next.

"Go back to Saigon with the men," said the doctor. "We're okay for the time being. They're sending another nurse to replace you . . . I gather you're needed at the hospital."

A flood of gratitude spread through Lee, and she hurried down the corridor to stand in line with the men for the flight home.

"I'm coming, Johnny, please be all right," she repeated inside.

It seemed an eternity before she was crammed on board the helicopter. It rose straight up in the air with trembles and roars and Lee talked to the men on board as patiently as she could. How long would it take? and would she find him when she got there? what would his condition be?

They flew through the starry night for a long time, and many of the men began to sleep. Lee was wide awake the whole time; she stared out the small window at the sky, which began to change to a deep blue with the coming dawn. It had been a long night, she realized, and it must have been midnight when she went out to find Johnny in the rice paddies. Now a new day was coming, and she saw a few lights down below and the Saigon river winding under the blue sky. The helicopter made its way across the tops of buildings and empty streets to the station hospital. Below Lee saw the playing field and more helicopters, and they began to descend.

As they did so, her heart rose in fear. She didn't want to know the truth again. It was too painful before; it would be painful again. She held her breath as they bounced onto the playing field. The men around her stirred and woke from slumber. The sky was royal blue, when they opened the door, and people were there to greet them and herd them into their hospital beds. Lee thought of the operating room; she was expected there very soon.

"Another load was brought in from the Mekong," she heard men saying around her. There would be a lot of work then.

She stepped onto the damp grass and walked with the men into the hospital. Some of them leaned on each other for support, but their faces all showed relief at being near civilization again.

Lee ran down the corridor of the hospital and saw the head nurse of the critical ward standing at her desk reading the daily newspaper. She smiled at Lee and put it down.

"Congratulations, Nurse Knight . . . We're all very proud of your bravery," she said.

"Thank you," Lee whispered, her voice catching on fear. "I wanted to ask you about one of the patients—Johnny Winston—"

"Oh yes. He's in there now," she said with a nod at the critical ward. "He's about to go into the operating room, then back to the States for further care."

"Can I go in?" Lee asked, still prepared for the worst.

"Of course," said the older woman. "And my congratulations again."

"Thank you."

Lee entered the white room, where each bed was concealed by a curtain. She peered into one and saw a stranger, and into the next. Johnny was lying there in a state of semi-consciousness, but when he saw Lee a shadow of his old wry smile appeared on his face.

"Hi, kid," he whispered.

Lee's eyes filled with tears and she went to his side and took his hands in hers. She leaned down and kissed his fingers, feeling weak with a mixture of happiness and sorrow. She gazed into his eyes, where pain was written, and she wondered when on earth they would meet again.

"You'll be all right," she said.

"And you?" he asked.

"I'll write to you."

"Not enough," he whispered, and his eyes closed.

She pushed the hair away from his damp forehead, just as two attendants arrived to take him to the operating room. Lee glanced at her watch and saw that it was time for her to work! Reluctantly she left Johnny with the men and ran down the hall to the nurse's station. She would be in the operating room with him, she realized, and so at least she would see his face again. She warded off the enormous sadness stored away inside of her, and went to the closet of the station to get out her uniform.

Just then the door opened and Khai came in.

* * *

The two girls stared at each other warily. Then Khai went to the closet and took out her coat; she was dressed in her uniform already.

"I had a call this morning, Lee," she said, "and so I must thank you for taking care of my mother."

"Where are you going?" Lee asked. "It's time for us to work!"

"I'm going home to join Khoung at the dispensary."

"But we need you here—"

"Then I'm going to work at the Vietnamese hospital— on a permanent basis. Hiem and I will live together. The phone call reported that Pham was badly injured. I must go to him."

"He's there? With Khoung?"

"No, Lee. Nearby."

Lee saw that behind the calm mask that Khai was wearing there hid a person on the verge of hysteria. She didn't know what to do, but she held out her hand to Khai. They looked at each other closely, until tears rose up in both of their visions. Khai accepted Lee's hand and held it tight.

"Take care, dear Lee," she said.

"You too."

"Some day we may meet in peace and be friends again."

"I hope so," Lee murmured.

They released hands and Khai left the room. Lee stood in silence for a moment, trying to control the terrible sadness she felt. Only the thought of Johnny in the operating room overcame it, and she hurried into her uniform as fast as she could.

Dr. Curtis and the nurse assisting him nodded at her when she entered. Johnny was on the table already, unconscious. Lee took her position and held her breath as the wound was exposed. It was very messy, but she had seen the same sort of thing before. The doctor would remove the shrapnel and the broken bones and provide a temporary suture for the broken tissue. In the hospital at home, he would receive intensive care to repair the damage to the internal organs that must have resulted from his wound.

Lee couldn't look at Johnny's face without wanting to cry, and so she pretended he was a stranger and performed her job with efficiency. Dr. Curtis seemed like a magician now. His calm and precision joined together to clean up the damage in a short time.

"He won't be in special forces again," the doctor said, when he had finished, "He'll need a new kidney."

"But he'll be all right?" Lee asked.

"Of course." The doctor glanced at his watch. "At one o'clock they'll have him on the jet home."

"I see," she murmured.

Johnny was taken away again and a new patient entered. Lee had to stay with the job, especially now that

Khai was gone. She controlled all her emotions, made worse by fatigue, and worked until noon. At that point she fled from the operating room back up to the critical ward. She drew back the curtains around his bed. It was empty.

Lee's knees began to shake. She clung to the curtains for support just as the nurse entered the ward.

"Are you all right?" the woman asked.

"Where did—did he go?" Lee asked.

"They've just taken him down to the field—"

"Excuse me. I must run."

Drawing a deep breath, Lee hurried into the corridor, where she didn't wait for the elevator. She ran down two flights of stairs to the back entrance of the hospital and flung open the door on a sunny day. A long stretch of green grass lay before her and she ran across it toward the group of helicopters that would take Johnny to the main airport. Ahead she saw a group of men and a couple of stretchers with people upon them.

"Johnny! Johnny!" her whole being cried.

And there he was, his green beret in his hands, lying down under a khaki blanket. He started to rise when he saw her, but a hand pushed him down again. He smiled and held out his hand to her, and she took it and held it against her.

"You made it, kid," he said in a low voice with a wince of pain.

The people around stared at them with small smiles, but they didn't interrupt. Lee leaned down and kissed Johnny's forehead and lips.

"Darling," she whispered, "I won't forget you ever."

"Forget me," he said with a grin. "You better not!"

"I'll be home a long time from now—"

"You get time off. You fly right back and see me."

"Okay," she said with a smile.

"I love you," he said.

The helicopter's propellor began to turn very slowly close by them.

"I love you too," she said desperately, "Forever."

"Better say goodbye," an officer warned her. "We're taking off."

Lee's eyes filled with tears and she kissed him on the lips again and again, until she felt him press his green beret into her hands. She looked at it in surprise.

"Pretend it's a ring. It means the same thing," Johnny said.

"When I come back—"

"We'll start a regular life," he said.

"I promise."

"Goodbye, Lee," he whispered and she saw his eyes fill with tears.

"Goodbye."

They hoisted him away from her on board the small helicopter, and he disappeared from sight. Lee turned away, blinded by tears, and faced the long green field and the hospital. She walked with dragging footsteps back to the place that was her only home now, and she clutched in her hands the green beret that would support her through the days to come.

At the door Maggie and Bennie were waiting for her. They put their arms around her and led her inside. She let her tears fall freely at last, for later she would have work to do. The present might hold nothing but sorrow, but the future held hopes of peace and joy. Even in the midst of sadness, she knew that better times would have to come. So many people wanted them.

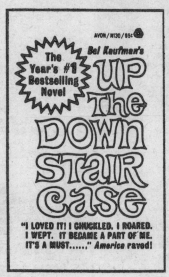